D1375194

Keith Moray is a part-time doctor, columnist and novelist. A member of the Crime Writers Association, the International Thriller Writers, and the Society of Authors, he lives and works in Wakefield.

DEATH IN TRANSIT

West Uist, Scotland. When a body is found
floating in Kyleshiffin harbour, it is unclear
whether there has been a tragic accident
or a cold-blooded murder. A chalked
astrological sign on the harbour wall
gathers significance when a second body
and another sign are discovered. This time
there is no doubt — it was murder most
foul. There is no shortage of suspects, with
tensions running high between the local
astronomical and astrological societies.
And the signs are that there will be more
deaths, unless Inspector Torquil McKinnon
and his team can solve the case and find
the zodiac killer.

Books by Keith Moray
Published by The House of Ulverscroft:

THE GATHERING MURDERS
DEATHLY WIND
MURDER SOLSTICE
FLOTSAM & JETSAM

KEITH MORAY

DEATH IN TRANSIT

Complete and Unabridged

ULVERSCROFT
Leicester

First published in Great Britain in 2013 by
Robert Hale Limited
London

First Large Print Edition
published 2014
by arrangement with
Robert Hale Limited
London

A catalogue record for this book is available
from the British Library.

ISBN 978–1–4448–2039–3

Published by
F. A. Thorpe (Publishing)
Anstey, Leicestershire

Set by Words & Graphics Ltd.
Anstey, Leicestershire
Printed and bound in Great Britain by
T. J. International Ltd., Padstow, Cornwall

This book is printed on acid-free paper

For my brother, George.
In admiration of his ability to hit
a controlled draw.
And, for my brother, John.
With fond memories of our hunt to
find the lost golf course at Rannoch.

Prologue

Watching the final painful death throes had been the worst experience imaginable. It had all been so quick to begin with and yet so interminable and . . .

The thoughts tumbled one after the other, each associated with a different emotion and yet some by the same emotion only more intensified. Anger, guilt, unbearable sorrow and hate. They all vied for momentary supremacy, but only served to keep the simmering pot of bitter resentment on target to boil over into undiluted rage.

Writing the book gave some solace. It was a different sort of book this time. A cookery book. Something to divert the mind; that had been the intention. Yet the allusions about cooking merely blurred the margins between creativity and a catastrophic breakdown.

For days, weeks and what seemed an everlasting sequence of months, the emotions bubbled away, never reducing as a good sauce would. Instead, they became concentrated, full-bodied and full-blooded.

And then slowly came clarification. Raw emotions slowly transformed the thoughts.

Realization came as a whole new theme presented itself in the writing of the book. Vengeance would be a tastier dish if served on a cool plate.

Revenge as a cold collation!

Seeing the article in a waiting-room magazine seemed entirely serendipitous. No, it seemed even more than that. A sign from the stars. How amusing and satisfying that thought was.

Murder in passing.

No, better still, death in transit.

It would just take some planning.

1

I

PC Ewan McPhee had been up since first light in order to get a couple of hours' training in before he opened up the Kyleshiffin station at eight. That had given him time for a quick breakfast and travel to and from the beach where he had managed a jog and a good forty minutes of hammer throwing. It was not that he had far to go, merely that his mode of transport was not suited to speed. But there again, West Uist was not a place where anything generally happened quickly.

'Hoi, Ewan McPhee!' cried Willie Staig, the bucolic newsagent, from his doorway as Ewan rode along Harbour Street on his mother's forty-year-old Norman Nippy 50cc moped. 'Is it not time that the West Uist Police shelled out for a squad car for you instead of that ancient motorized hobby-horse!'

Ewan grinned and waved a large hand in dismissal for he was well used to gentle teasing from the local folk. He had to admit that the sight of a big, six-foot-four, red-haired police constable riding such a machine was not without its comic appeal.

He rode on, waving to several of the market folk who were busily setting up their stalls and wares alongside the harbour sea-wall. He sighed with contentment for he truly loved the familiar multicoloured shop-fronts of the crescent-shaped Harbour Street, the flotilla of yachts, cabin cruisers and fishing boats that bobbed up and down in the harbour itself.

Most of all though, he loved being the junior officer of the West Uist branch of the Hebridean Constabulary. It was the smallest police force in the country, consisting of his friends, Inspector Torquil McKinnon, Sergeant Morag Driscoll and himself. In addition, there were two special constables, the Drummond twins, who were technically subordinate to Ewan when they were on duty, although for most of the time they did what they pleased, only helping out when Torquil or Morag put pressure on them to do so.

His thoughts were broken by the sound of a marine horn sounding out three times from beyond the harbour. He looked round to see *Neptune's Trident*, the Drummond twins' old fishing boat, chugging out to sea. He could make out both of them standing in the cabin gesticulating at him rudely.

'The impudent pair,' he grunted, being too

conscious of his position as a police officer to retaliate. Yet despite himself he grinned. Everyone on the island knew the Drummond twins and most just accepted their rough and ready ways. They were island fishermen born and bred, and special police constables by inclination. Like their father and grandfather before them, they were part of West Uist's inshore fishing fleet.

Och, they're just a couple of rogues, he mused to himself. Maybe I'll get them to wash down the *Seaspray* as a punishment. They don't like anything that involves honest elbow grease.

As he made his way along the road towards MacOnachie's Chandlery, which stood at the head of the stairs leading down to the quay, he spotted Tam MacOnachie himself leaning against the sea wall. He was a man of about seventy with weather-beaten skin and a ring of hair around his head that gave the bald dome above it the look of a boiled egg. Indeed, it was for that reason that the Drummond twins had nicknamed him 'Eggy' MacOnachie, much to his annoyance and their glee. He was not one of their many fans.

He was wearing his usual brown shop-coat with an oiled apron on top and with his trousers tucked into his aged wellington boots. He was lowering a pair of binoculars from his eyes. He waved Ewan down and the big constable stopped.

'Did you see them, Constable McPhee?' he cried with exasperation. 'It's lucky they were out of the harbour or I would reprimand them. That's no way for police officers to behave.'

'You should give them a ticking-off anyway, Mr MacOnachie,' Ewan called back. 'You are the harbour master and they could do with a lesson. But technically, when they are in their boat they are fishermen, not police officers.'

Tam MacOnachie grunted and stuffed his binoculars into a pocket of his coat. 'I'll do just that. Aye, and maybe I will complain to Inspector McKinnon.'

Ewan gave a non-committal shrug, which was greeted with a scowl before Eggy MacOnachie flounced off into his chandlery. Ewan grinned as he started off again and headed up the street.

Tam MacOnachie had been the harbour master for as long as Ewan could remember and he had a definite puritanical streak. The thought of him reprimanding the twins was even better than his idea of getting them to wash down the police launch.

'Mercy me!' he exclaimed as he turned up Kirk Wynd, which ran parallel to Harbour

Street, and gave Nippy a helping hand by pedalling for all he was worth. 'It is going to be a scorcher of a day. I only hope that it will be a quiet day because of it.'

He drew up outside the converted pebble-dashed cottage that was the Kyleshiffin police station and pulled Nippy onto its stand. It was then that he noticed the figure waiting on the far side of the doorway, behind the separate notice-board that they used for all the official police bulletins and notices. His heart sank as he recognized the figure.

He silently mouthed a prayer, for he suspected that his hope of a quiet day was going to be a forlorn one.

II

Torquil McKinnon had been in a depressed mood the previous evening after he had seen his fiancée, Sergeant Lorna Golspie, off on the overnight ferry to Oban. Ever since they had begun their relationship the previous summer, their boss, Superintendent Lumsden, had seemed intent upon keeping them apart. Neither of them were in any doubt about his motivation for doing so since he and Torquil had some history.

After a frugal breakfast with his uncle, the

7

Reverend Lachlan McKinnon, they had gone their separate ways; Lachlan to the local golf course while Torquil prepared to ride out to St Ninian's Cave.

'Come on, Crusoe,' he said, clapping the side of his leg and clicking his tongue, sending the young tri-coloured collie that gambolled at his feet into a tail-wagging frenzy. He crunched across the gravel forecourt of the manse, where he and his uncle had lived ever since Torquil's parents had drowned in a boating accident in the Minch when Torquil was a youngster, and Lachlan had become his guardian.

In one hand Torquil carried his old Cromwell helmet and in the other he held his bagpipes. He stuffed the latter into one of the panniers on his classic Royal Enfield Bullet 500cc motorcycle. He whistled and nodded his head and Crusoe obediently leapt up onto the seat before allowing Torquil to lower him into the other pannier. Torquil pulled on his helmet, goggles and gauntlets and wound his McKinnon tartan scarf about his neck before pulling the machine off its stand.

'A good play on the pipes is what I need, Crusoe,' he said to the dog. 'So it is a trip to St Ninian's Cave and the bay where I first found you strapped to that piece of drift-wood.'

He pursed his lips as the dog's ears

8

flattened, almost as if it understood what was being said to him. Then he grinned and tousled Crusoe's head. 'Cheer up, my wee pal. I'll soon lift both our spirits with a couple of reels and maybe a strathspey.'

And mounting the motorcycle he switched on the ignition and then kick-started it into action.

Minutes later they were hurtling round the chicane-like coastal road, gunning the Bullet's engine and scattering myriads of gulls from the machair and sand dunes between them and the sea, sending them flying protestingly towards the stacks and skerries that were so typical along the West Uist coast.

Soon the great sea cave came into view and his spirits started to rise.

III

Sergeant Morag Driscoll was not due into work until 8.30, but felt in need of the distraction of work and a bit of company. It was the middle of the school holidays and she had taken the opportunity to send her three children off on holiday to France with her sister and her family. Ordinarily that would have filled her with joy at having time to spend on her own, but since she had recently started a relationship with Sandy King, the celebrated Scottish international footballer, and he had returned to the mainland on the overnight ferry after a delightful weekend together, she found herself pining.

An attractive thirty-something, single mother of three, Morag fought a continual battle with her weight; it was not that she was at all overweight, but because she had lost her husband to an unexpected heart attack when she was only twenty-six. Accordingly, she had determined to do all that she could in order to minimize her own risk, for she had no intention of allowing her children to become orphaned.

Passing Allardyce, the bakery, she was suddenly assailed by the aroma of freshly baked butter rolls and succumbed to the temptation.

Ewan will manage a couple, I am sure, she thought to herself.

There was a short queue already and she joined it. After a few moments the door opened and more people came in. She turned and found herself standing in front of a pretty young woman in her early twenties with short crinkly hair and with large hoop earrings. She was dressed in jeans with fashionable holes in the knees, pink trainers and a T-shirt with the logo 'The West Uist Chronicle WRITES!'

'Good morning, Cora,' she greeted her. 'An early start at the *Chronicle* is it?'

Cora Melville smiled and made a mock gesture of rubbing her eyes. 'And a good morning to you too, Sergeant Driscoll,' she replied cheerfully. 'Actually it is a late night that I have just had. Calum has been getting a special issue of the paper together. It is about all the star folk who have descended on the island. He says that we need to keep a step ahead of Scottish TV and the glossy magazines.'

Morag nodded knowingly. 'Ah, trust Calum to keep a step ahead of the opposition. And I know what you mean about folk flooding into West Uist. Our telephone has barely stopped, with people ringing up and asking if we know of anywhere to stay. All the hotels and B&Bs seem full up. You would think that the police station had turned into an accommodation centre.' She shook her head. 'So are you enjoying working with our local newshound?'

Cora's cheeks flushed. 'We get on really well, Sergeant.' She smiled then let out an effervescent giggle. 'Oh, excuse me. It is just that it still seems a bit odd working for your boyfriend.'

'Lucky you, Cora,' Morag replied with a wistful smile. 'My chap Sandy has to be in

11

Glasgow all week and has an important match on Saturday.'

'So it is going well with you two, is it, Sergeant?'

'I wish you would call me Morag. Aye, it is. I never expected to have another man in my life again, but it is just — lovely.'

'Maybe it was written in the stars, Morag.'

Morag smiled. 'Aye, maybe. So tell me, what is your take on all this star business? As you say, the island seems to have had a real flood of folk with telescopes and binoculars.'

'Ah, those are the astronomy lot.' Cora looked about her as if wary of eavesdroppers in the queue. Then she went on in a half whisper, 'There's also the new age brigade. They are the astrologers. You can usually tell them apart. The astronomers are the intellectual-looking ones with anoraks, beards, bow ties and specs. The new age astrology types are starry-eyed and wear baggy clothes, beads and bangles.'

Morag laughed. 'And just why are they all coming to the island now?'

'It is this transit of Mercury and a weird pattern of the planets that is about to happen.'

Morag raised her eyebrows vacantly. 'And — er — what is a transit of Mercury? I should be paying more attention to what's going on, but I've sort of had my head in the clouds lately.'

Cora giggled, 'Actually, I didn't know either, Morag. It means that the planet Mercury is about to travel across between the sun and the Earth. And as it does it apparently kisses Venus on the way. That's called a conjunction. It doesn't happen very often.'

The queue moved ahead and a couple of customers squeezed past them on their way out. They edged forward.

'So have they all come to watch it?'

'The astronomers have, the astrology folk have come to feel it.'

'Feel it? That sounds a bit freaky.'

'It does a bit, doesn't it? But apparently it is all to do with the unique position of West Uist. We have virtually no light pollution here so it is an astronomical clear spot and the astronomers will get one of the best possible views as it passes in front of the sun. You can't look directly at it through a telescope, though, or you could scorch your eyes. You have to rig up your telescope to see a reflection. That's one of the things we've written about. As for the new age people, well they think that . . . '

She hesitated as if trying to find the right words. 'They think there is something mystical about the island and something weird may be about to happen.'

Morag grimaced. 'Oh dear, we have had folk obsessed with the solstice before.'

Another couple of customers squeezed past them and they moved up to the counter where Gordon Allardyce and his assistant Freddie Mason were serving.

'Good morning, ladies,' Gordon greeted them, as he rinsed his plastic-gloved hands and shook them dry. 'And what can I be getting you this fine morning? Baps, rolls, sandwiches of your choice, or how about our latest line — transit pasties?'

'Oh, not you, too, Gordon!' Morag said with a smile and a shake of her head. 'Is this you cashing in on the star people?'

Gordon Allardyce, a ruddy-faced, middle-aged bachelor and a notorious flirt, winked at Morag. 'I am always in favour of anything to do with Venus, the goddess of love, Morag Driscoll.' He grinned good-humouredly then went on with mock innocence. 'Did I hear that your boyfriend is away playing football all week? Maybe you will be feeling a bit lonely.'

'Away with you, Gordon. You are a rogue,' Morag returned with equal good humour. 'Just give me four butter rolls and a bit less of the flirtation.'

Gordon's bottom lip fell in crestfallen fashion. 'But are you sure you won't try a transit pastie? I won't be doing the line for long. After this transit that they're all on about the line will be finished.'

Morag pouted. 'Oh, you had better give me three as well, then.' Immediately she felt guilty about the purchase and a bit piqued at herself for being persuaded to buy what she didn't need. She made a mental note to go for a run in the evening.

As she waited for Gordon to bag up her purchases her mobile phone beeped to tell her that she had a text. She pulled it out of her belt holster and smiled with glee when she saw it was from Sandy. Her eyebrows rose as she read it:

Watch out for Venus tonight, darling. It is supposed to be a good night for love!

She suppressed a sigh. Sandy King had shown himself to be a big romantic, completely at variance with the tough, hard-man image that he projected on the football field.

'I'll be seeing you then, Morag,' Cora said, as she collected her two bulging paper bags from Freddie Mason and paid the exact amount from her purse. 'I had better get these over to Calum. We'll see what he makes of these transit pasties.'

Gordon Allardyce clicked his tongue as he

handed Morag her bags. 'There you go, Morag Driscoll,' he said with a wink. 'Everybody likes a bit of Venus. Even Calum Steele.'

IV

Torquil had parked in the lay-by above St Ninian's Bay then jumped down with Crusoe and scrunched across the shingle beach to the entrance of St Ninian's Cave. While Torquil walked inside Crusoe went scampering around, exploring the rock pools and piles of seaweed.

The great basalt-columned cave had been used by generations of island pipers, including Torquil's uncle Lachlan. He remembered the day when he had taken him and his pipes and introduced him to the cave's special magic. The young Torquil had hoped that he would one day follow in his uncle's footsteps and become a champion piper and winner of the Silver Quaich. Much to their mutual pleasure he duly did, so that there now resided a Silver Quaich on each end of the mantelpiece in the manse's sitting-room.

Nature had carved this sea cave beautifully and it seemed to hold a sound perfectly for a moment so that the piper was able to hear the correct pitch of his playing. It was a natural tape recorder for a musician.

For ten minutes he ran through his repertoire of warm-up exercises, to get his finger movements right. He played a string of ever more complex movements — *leumluaths*, *taorluaths*, grace notes and birls. Then he played a couple of reels and a strathspey. And then, since he felt he was playing well, he concentrated on one of his own latest compositions, a *piobaireachd*, the *pibroch*.

It was a Torquil in much higher spirits who emerged from the cave some while later. Crusoe spied him at once, barked then sprinted over to gambol round his ankles in sheer delight.

'Ah, the air is good this morning and the sea looks tempting, doesn't it, boy?'

Bending down he picked up a piece of driftwood and flung it over the waves. Crusoe gave a yelp of pleasure then bounded into the surf and swam towards the stick.

Torquil laughed and shielded his eyes with his hand to watch the dog. Then suddenly Crusoe started to bark and instead of swimming towards the wood he started swimming in circles.

'What's wrong, Crusoe, have you lost interest?'

Crusoe continued to bark and swim in circles.

'Are you trying to tell me something, boy?'
Then he saw the source of Crusoe's agitation.
Far off, just near the outlines of the Cruadalach Isles in the far distance he fancied he
spied movement.

He reached into his pocket and drew out
the monocular mini-telescope that he always
carried and trained it on the shapes.

'*Creideamh*! Faith!' he exclaimed. 'Kayakers, three of them and one seems to be in
trouble.'

They were clearly well out of earshot, but
by the way one of them was thrashing about
it looked as though they had either capsized
or somehow started to sink. They had obviously ignored the warning buoys that marked
the underwater skerries on the approach to
the Cruadalachs, some of which were as sharp
as claymore swords and could slash the bottom
out of a canoe or kayak. I had better let them
know that they've been spotted and then I'll
get help to them, he mused.

He whistled. 'I see them, Crusoe. You come
back in now.'

Raising his blowpipe to his lips he blew
up the bag and played a series of rapid
leumluaths and *taorluaths* at full blast. In the
open air the Great Highland Bagpipe was
better than any siren.

Looking through the monocular again he

saw one of the kayakers waving frantically. 'Good, that's got their attention,' he said, laying his pipes down on the beach just as Crusoe emerged from the water and started to shake his coat.

'Good boy!' Torquil said, patting him vigorously and prompting a wag of the tail.

Torquil pulled out his mobile phone and rang the station. 'It is an emergency, Crusoe,' he said to the dog, as he listened to the dialling tone. 'I just hope that none of the island's chatterboxes is keeping Ewan from answering the station phone this morning.'

V

Ewan had unlocked the station door and let in his first customer. He barely had time to get behind the desk and close the counter flap before the man stomped in behind him. He was dressed in waterproofs with a baseball cap perched on a large head. An unlit cigar was clenched between his teeth and in his hand he held a scrunched-up piece of paper.

'It is an outrage!' he growled, tossing the paper down on the counter. 'What are you going to do about it, that's what I want to know?'

Ewan picked up the paper and smoothed it

out. 'So you've been fined, Mr McDonald,' he said. 'It looks clear enough. You'll need to pay the harbour master twenty-five pounds.'

'I will not! That fool Tam MacOnachie is just an officious oaf. He has no right sticking these . . . these parking tickets on my boat. I want to charge him.'

'Mr McDonald, as you well know, the harbour is outside our jurisdiction. Tam MacOnachie is in charge and if you have been using the wrong harbour berth he is entitled — '

'Entitled to nothing! Well, if you won't do something about it, this is what I think.' He snatched the paper from Ewan and tore it in pieces then threw it in the air. He turned on his heel and stomped for the door. 'And if he doesn't like it, he can sue me. I've used that harbour for years and I'll continue to do so wherever I see fit. What's he doing with these new rules?'

Ewan opened his mouth to reply, but Ming McDonald had gone. With a shrug he reached for his tea.

The ring of the telephone prevented him from slaking his thirst.

'Morning, Torquil,' he said. 'What can I — ?' His eyes opened wide with alarm and he reached for his pencil to take details of the emergency.

20

2

I

The Reverend Lachlan McKinnon — known locally as the Padre — had been a single handicap golfer for all of his adult life and was pleased that he could still manage to play to a handicap of eight, just under an eighth of his age.

Lord, it is good to be alive on a day like this, he mused to himself, as he strode towards his ball in the middle of the third fairway. If I can still thump the ball a good two hundred and fifty yards like this for the medal competition on Saturday I will have a good chance.

Lachlan was proud of the ten-acre plot of undulating dunes and machair that he and several other local worthies had years before transformed into the St Ninian's Golf Course. Using the natural lie of the land they had constructed six holes, each with at least two potential hazards. The fairways were tractor-mown once a week, the greens were sheep-grazed to near billiard table smoothness and the bunkers had been excavated by generations of rabbits. Each hole had three separate tee positions, each one giving its route to the hole a special name in both English and Gaelic, thereby allowing players the choice of playing a conventional eighteen holes or any combination they chose.

He was a tall man with a mop of shaggy white hair that seemed to defy the application of brush or comb, who sported a pair of horn-rimmed spectacles. He was dressed in his usual attire which he wore both on and off the golf course; a green West Uist tweed jacket, corduroy trousers, black shirt and a dog collar. It was his custom to play the first three holes then pop into his church, St Ninian's, which overlooked the third green. Since he had actually been the course architect some of his golfing cronies often jibbed that he had designed it that way to get extra help from his heavenly employer.

'Now let's see if I can make the green and set up a birdie chance,' he said, relishing having the course all to himself.

He set his bag on the ground and selected his eight iron, the club that he was deadly with from virtually any lie from 120 yards or less. He took his position, made a couple of practice waggles then swung easily through the ball. The result pleased him no end as he watched the ball sail up over the ridge then drop and roll on the soft green to land a couple of feet from the hole.

He paused a moment to fill a battered old briar pipe from a yellow oilskin pouch, then struck a light and soon had it going to his satisfaction.

Minutes later he was on the green, tapping his putt into the hole.

As he bent to pick it out of the cup he heard someone clap their hands. A cheery voice called out, 'Ha! Not even a golfing minister could miss one that close.' It was followed by a deep chuckle.

Lachlan collected the ball then straightened and turned towards the church. The sun was shining directly in his eyes and he had to squint to see who his spectator was.

A striking-looking man of about Lachlan's age was standing in the church porch. He was slimly built, some three or four inches shorter than Lachlan, with a narrow goatee beard and iron-grey hair swept straight back to hang at collar length and with an eye patch over his left eye. With an off-white cotton suit and a flamboyant, old-fashioned bow tie, he had the look of a Buffalo Bill Cody or some other latter-day showman. With another chuckle he walked down the path to the small iron gate and let himself onto the course.

'Murdoch!' Lachlan cried, advancing to meet him with his hand extended. 'You are early. I was not expecting you to arrive on the island until this evening. This heavenly happening of yours is not due until tomorrow, is it?'

'The conjunction of Venus and Mercury and the transit of Mercury,' returned Murdoch Jamieson, Scottish TV's very own astronomy presenter on the *Heavens Above* programme. 'Then later we'll be filming the conjunction of Jupiter and Uranus. It is all a very different heavenly concern than the dubious stuff that you peddle, Lachlan.'

'Still the devout atheist, I see!' Lachlan retorted. 'You haven't changed a bit since our university days. And I see that you still always put a wee atheistic jibe in on your TV show.'

Murdoch looked scandalized. 'A show! It is a popular science documentary slot, if you don't mind, you old reprobate.'

Lachlan absently reached for his pipe in his front breast pocket and tapped the remaining tobacco out against the blade of his putter. 'Aye, if you say so, Murdoch. Although the thing that puzzles me is how you have managed to keep talking about astronomy for all these years. How long has the show — er, I mean the programme, been running now? It must be what, twenty-eight or twenty-nine years or so?'

'The conjunction and transit will mark my thirtieth anniversary with Scottish TV. I am going to go out on a high note, Lachlan. I'm going to retire this year.'

'Retire? But you are a national institution, man. You can no more retire than I can. Surely you are kidding me?'

'I was never more serious, Lachlan. I think I am getting past my sell-by date. Look at me; I am a bit of a dinosaur, an elegant one I will admit, yet a dinosaur none the less. I used to be considered chic, but nowadays they want smart young physics professors with pop-star looks or glamorous female presenters with a doctorate or two. I am just one of the old school of science boffins with a simple, general degree and I plan to go before the television company ask me to leave.'

Lachlan pointed towards the gate. 'I will believe it when I see it, Murdoch. In the meanwhile, shall I show you the top of the tower?'

'Lead on, Macduff!' replied Murdoch, holding his hand out for Lachlan to pass. 'I'll bet this is the first time that old tower of yours has been used as an observatory for serious scientific research.'

Lachlan led the way up the gravel path and leaned his clubs against the wall in the porch before opening the heavy old church door.

'As a matter of fact it is a first, Murdoch. Yet there are two other reasons I am pleased that you are going to be filming from here.'

'Enlighten me. Minister!'

Lachlan closed the door behind them then stood chuckling. 'Well, not only will I be getting you inside a church for the first time in forty years, but St Ninian's Church is special. It stands on top of a much older pagan site.'

He pointed to the standing stone with its peculiar ancient markings, that stood behind the baptismal font. 'You see, the church was built in the eighth century, but the stone was here long before that. They just built the church around it. It was a common-enough practice to build churches on top of old pagan sites.'

Murdoch gave a slow smile and, reaching out, touched and ran a finger over part of a pattern on the stone. It was covered in carvings; a mix of curls, wavy lines, straight lines and with one or two carvings suggestive of human forms. 'It looks pagan right enough, Lachlan. These are like runes.'

'That's why I wanted you to see it, Murdoch. I thought it might bring you some proper enlightenment. The stone is called *Eilthireach*, the Pilgrim Stone.'

This amused Murdoch. He tossed his head back and laughed heartily. 'Is that what you thought, Lachlan? That I am here on a pilgrimage? That I might be converted to the faith?'

Lachlan gave him a mock punch on the

arm. 'It was worth a try. Now come on, let me show you our tower.'

II

Calum Steele leaned back in his editorial chair, savouring one of Gordon Allardyce's transit pasties.

'Not bad, Cora lassie. Not bad.' He winked at her from behind his wire-framed spectacles and took a hefty gulp of lukewarm tea. 'Not as good as his mutton pies, but I admire Tam's enterprising spirit in cashing in on this planetary gobbledy-gook.'

Calum was a short, tubby man of twenty-eight who had managed to sail through his adult life paying little attention to fashion until he had started going out with Cora Melville, when she had begun to work for him as his assistant reporter.

'Oh, Calum!' Cora chided him. 'How can you say that when we spent half of the night writing all those articles explaining about the transit of Mercury and the conjunctions from both an astronomical and an astrological view?'

Calum sighed. 'That is the nature of journalism, Cora. You don't have to be remotely interested in the stuff you write, you just have to be interested in producing something that

27

keeps the public reading your paper.'

'But you taught me that — '

'Och, I say a lot of things, lassie. And you will note that I can usually justify every one of those things.'

'Well, y . . . yes, you seem to, but — '

'It is sophistry, Cora. Journalistic sophistry. Just like those ancient Greek chappies, *the Sophists* they were called, you have to learn to argue from any point of view.'

He swivelled his chair round and pointed to the desk — 'the working editor's desk', as he always referred to it with his customary aplomb in his column. It was covered in reams of paper, open books and lots of scribbled Post-it notes. On the left of the desk stood an old, battered and coffee-stained computer with a keyboard that was so well used most of the keys had lost their letters. On the right side was Calum's trusty laptop, and between them both was a dusty old Remington typewriter.

'Look at all these things, Cora. The paraphernalia of the writer's craft: pens, pencils, my old typewriter and now all the latest technology. What does it all say to you?'

Cora pouted thoughtfully. 'That we are journalists? That this is the office of the *West Uist Chronicle?*'

Calum waved his hand encouragingly, as if

28

he was turning a handle in the air. 'Good, good, but what are all these things?'

He smiled knowingly, then went on before Cora had time to reply, 'They are just tools, Cora. Just tools of the trade. On their own they are useless.' He tapped the side of his head with a stubby forefinger. 'It is our genius for words that makes the tools work, lassie. You must remember that. It isn't the pen that is mightier than the sword, it's the person who knows how to use it.'

He leaned back and hooked his thumbs behind his braces and beamed. 'Do you see what I mean?'

Cora eyed the braces with disdain, for although she realized that Calum thought they enhanced his image as an editor, she had earmarked them as one of the first things that she was going to change in her boyfriend. But she was prepared to choose her moment to broach the subject.

A bell rang downstairs, indicating that someone had entered the *Chronicle's* reception room.

'Shop!' called an assertive female voice. 'Is there anyone serving here?'

Calum shot forward with indignation and silently mouthed the word *shop*!

'What do they think this is? A newsagent's?' he whispered. He pushed himself up to his full five foot six inches and pulled in his stomach. 'I'll give them *shop*!'

But before he had taken a step there was the sound of jangling metal and of leather-heeled boots coming quickly up the bare wooden stairs.

'Ah, people!' said an attractive and stylish woman of about fifty dressed in a multi-coloured, almost psychedelic dress. She seemed to be wearing at least six different necklaces and multiple bangles on each wrist, accounting for the jangling as she moved. She had a mass of long, curly auburn hair, held in place by a scarlet headband and also by a pair of designer sunglasses thrust into the mass of hair like an Alice band. She was every inch the gracefully ageing hippy.

She stood staring at Calum and Cora for a moment then smiled graciously and raised a hand in which she grasped the latest issue of the *West Uist Chronicle*.

'One of you must be the editor!' It was a statement rather than a question. Then she snapped her fingers. 'Ah, it must be you, my dear little man.'

Calum's mouth fell open and he stammered a reply. 'Aye, th — that's me. Calum Steele at your service, This is my assistant, Cora Melville.'

The woman nodded her head with a smile. 'I am Dr Janet Horne and I am here for the event. I expect that you have heard of me. I am giving a series of lectures on the astrological houses, planetary relationships and their predictive power. They have been organized by your local celebrity, Dr Mathieson, and the West Uist Astrological Society.'

Calum almost spluttered at the thought of Melissa Mathieson the candlemaker as a celebrity, local or otherwise. He quickly put on his professional journalist's mask. 'Oh aye, Dr Horne. Pleased to meet you. We have an advert about your lectures in the paper.'

'Which I read this morning at breakfast. I am at the Masonic Arms Hotel in case you need to know that later, for interview purposes. I expect that you will want to have an expert astrological opinion.'

'Oh — er, that would be an idea, maybe.'

'Which brings me to the purpose of my visit. It is to congratulate you on this excellent paper and your wonderful column.'

Calum beamed at Cora.

'And which particular column did you have in mind, Dr Horne?'

Doctor Horne opened the paper to show the long column on page four. There was a graphic of a birth chart heading it. 'This wonderful horoscope column, of course, by your consultant astrologer — Denarius, I think you call him.' She peered at the name and tapped the paper. 'Yes, Denarius. A clever choice of name, I have to admit. So evocative of the augurs of ancient Rome.'

Calum and Cora exchanged a look of bemusement.

'I would love you to introduce me to him. I take it that it is a him?'

Calum hesitated for a moment, then: 'Oh, aye, he's a him all right.'

'Well let me just say that he is so accurate! His column today is exactly what I would have written. Anyway, I take it you will be coming to my first lecture tonight?'

Cora was quick to chip in. 'He will. We both will.'

'Excellent! Tonight it is then. The more people who realize the importance of what is about to happen, the better. 'Bye.'

She exited as she had entered with a staccato noise of heels on the wooden stairs accompanied by the jangling of metal jewellery.

'Calum, I didn't realize we had a consultant astrologer?' Cora queried once the bell rang to indicate that Dr Horne had left the building.

Calum pushed his spectacles back on his nose. 'We don't, lassie. You see, I am Denarius.'

Cora stared at him for a moment, then jackknifed forward and let out one of her belly laughs of delight.

When she had recovered, she asked, 'So

how do you know so much about astrology? I would never have thought it was something you were into, Calum.'

'Actually, Cora, I don't know anything, really. It's all mumbo-jumbo, if you ask me. I just make it up,'

'And what about the name?'

'I wrote an article about coin-collecting once. A denarius is a wee silver Roman coin, I liked the sound of it. But I hope you see my point; a good journalist gives the people what the people want, even if it is all bananas.'

Cora shook her head in disbelief and wonder, then again burst into a peal of irresistible laughter that ensnared Calum and soon they were both in hysterics.

They were laughing so much that they almost didn't hear the harbour master's siren going off. When they did Calum immediately moved into action. He grabbed his well-worn yellow anorak, his digital camera and his notebook.

'Come on, Cora, Tam MacOnachie is telling us we have a story to cover. No rest for investigative journalists.'

III

'It is a grand view that you have from here, Lachlan,' Murdoch Jamieson said, as he leaned on the stone curtain wall at the top of the tower. 'You can see for miles.'

Lachlan laughed. 'It is when we have cloudless skies, which as you know is not all that often. The Hebrides are renowned for their weather and here on West Uist we get squalls that whip up in a moment.'

He spoke with the enthusiasm of a man who was content with his lot in life. 'Aye, but for all the wind and rain that we get I wouldn't want to live anywhere else.' He pointed to the wind vane. 'If you were a bird and you followed the direction of the wee breeze that's ruffling your hair just now, you wouldn't touch land until you hit America.'

Murdoch raised a hand and adjusted his eye patch slightly. He had lost his left eye in a shinty match when he and Lachlan had been at university together. 'I can't see America, though, Lachlan.'

Lachlan chuckled. 'Didn't Nelson say something about not seeing ships at Trafalgar?'

'It was the Battle of Copenhagen, Lachlan, as I suspect you know. I wondered how long it would be before you came out with an Admiral Nelson joke.'

'Forgive me, old friend. I haven't seen you for a few years and I've been itching to tell some of the old jokes. You can hardly be sensitive about it though, can you? After all, having that eye patch has been your greatest asset in your career. There can't be too many one-eyed astronomers on TV.'

There was the sound of a door opening from the bottom of the tower then hesitant footsteps starting up the stairs.

'Murdoch? Are you there?'

'I'm up here,' Murdoch answered. 'Just come on up. I'm having a blether with the Padre.'

A few moments later a young man of about thirty with a prodigious belly, closely cropped hair, designer stubble and a dangly earring came puffing up the stairs. He was wearing a faded bomber jacket and underneath it a T-shirt with a picture of a star map enclosing the pattern of the W-shaped constellation Cassiopeia above the words *Heavens Above*, the logo of Murdoch's show. Under one arm he had a large bag and under the other he had a series of metal tubes that was unmistakably a collapsed tripod. On his back he had a rucksack packed with other electronic equipment. He lowered his various bundles to the floor then wiped his brow on a sleeve.

'Jings, it's hot today, Murdoch,' he said with a grin. 'Thank goodness for this breeze.'

Murdoch laughed. 'It's not all that hot, Gavin, you devil. Don't pretend it's the heat that's making you perspire. It's all that beer that you stow away in that five-gallon belly of

35

yours.' And as Gavin began to protest Murdoch tapped him on the arm and winked with his good eye.

'Calm yourself, Gavin. This is my old friend the Reverend Lachlan McKinnon and this is his church that he's lending us for the show, so no — '

' — I know, no swearing,' replied Gavin, with a good-natured grin as he shook hands with Lachlan.

'There's a box downstairs in the church if Murdoch drives you to the odd curse,' said Lachlan. 'Contributions are always welcome.'

'I guess you know what he puts me through, then?' Gavin joked.

'I do. I was at university with him.'

Gavin grinned and took a step towards the curtain wall. 'It's a grand view, right enough. You can see all the way out to those little islands. And that boat is — !'

He grabbed the top of the wall and screwed up his eyes. 'Bloody hell!'

'That'll cost you, Gavin,' Murdoch began with a grin.

But Gavin had dropped to one knee and started pulling a camera with a huge tele-photo lens from his bag. 'There's some sort of emergency going on out there, I think. Better try and catch it on film. It could be worth a spot on the news.'

Lachlan and Murdoch were watching as with deft efficiency Gavin swung his camera round to focus on the distant scene.

'I know that boat. It's the Drummond boys!' Lachlan said. 'It looks as if they're playing good Samaritans today out at the Cruadalach Isles.'

He did not see Murdoch eyeing him askance. Nor did he see the scowl on his face.

IV

Wallace had been at the wheel when the harbour siren started to blast out and moments later they received the distress call for help at the Cruadalach Isles. They sped off at full speed.

Douglas stood outside with his binoculars to his eyes.

'Go canny as we get close,' he said a few minutes later as they homed in towards the small archipelago of islets.

'Can you see them?'

'Aye, there seem to be three kayakers. Looks like one of them holed their boat. They have all made it to the isle, at any rate. They are safe.'

'Righto! We don't want to scuttle our inheritance,' Wallace returned with a grin.

'The old boy's spirit would never forgive us if we scuttled *Neptune's Trident*.'

A few moments later they coasted in towards the largest of the Cruadalach Isles where three kayakers were standing waiting for them, one of whom, a blonde-haired young woman in her mid-twenties, was shivering despite an emergency foil rescue blanket that she had pulled around herself.

'Everyone safe?' Douglas called out, as he vaulted into the shallows and waded ashore in his big fishermen's boots. 'We are the West Uist Police.'

'The police?' the younger of the two men repeated with a tone of disbelief tinged with disdain. He had a port-wine birthmark over the right side of his forehead and around his eye.

'Aye, that's what I said,' Douglas returned good-humouredly. 'We are special constables masquerading as fishermen.'

'Well, thank goodness you came so quickly,' said the woman. 'We heard someone belting out with a bagpipes from West Uist and didn't expect a rescue so soon.'

The twins looked at each other and grinned. 'That bagpiper is our boss, Inspector Torquil McKinnon. He must have been having an early morning practice at St Ninian's Cave. It seems he saw you then alerted the station, then the station alerted the harbour master and he sent us.'

'Did you spring a leak or something?' Wallace asked from the boat.

The older man, an athletic-looking fellow of about forty, nodded. 'Rosie here must have gashed the bottom of her kayak on an underwater rock.' He pointed to the two kayaks that had been hauled up on the beach and at the other still in the shallows, its cockpit full of water.

'Aye, there are a lot of needles of rock lurking about the Cruadalach Isles. Did you not see the warning buoys?'

'What buoys?' asked the younger man sarcastically.

The Drummond twins both looked out to sea and frowned in unison.

'What the devil?' said Wallace.

'Streuth!' exclaimed Douglas. 'They have all gone.'

'Do you mean those buoys?' the older man asked.

The twins followed his pointing finger to a pile of buoys lying behind a small sand dune.

'Jings!' said Douglas as he walked over to inspect them. 'They had washed ashore. That's curious.'

He knelt and examined them, whistled softly and then stood and turned. 'Well, folks,

I think we had better get you all back to West Uist.' He smiled at the girl. 'Especially you, miss. You don't want to be catching a chill.'

Wallace did not fail to see the puppy-dog stare that his brother was prone to when smitten by a bonny lass. He inwardly cringed, for he was all too familiar with the signs that suggested that Douglas was about to lose his heart and head. It was a not-infrequent occurrence.

'We'll need to drag my kayak out first and bail it out,' she said.

'I'll see to it in a minute, miss. Let me help you aboard first.'

He held out his hand towards her, but the younger man moved faster. He put a territorial arm about her shoulder. 'I'll see to Rosie, *Special Constable*,' he said, ushering her towards the fishing boat rope ladder. 'Why don't you help Henry to retrieve and bail out the kayak?'

Five minutes later they were steering a course back to West Uist. The twins were standing next to each other in the bridge, while the rescued party were sitting in the stern drinking tea laced with a drop of Glen Corlan from Douglas's hip flask — for medicinal purposes, he had explained.

'Well?' Wallace whispered. 'What did you find?'

'The buoy ropes had all been cut.'

Wallace bit his lip. 'Whoever did that has a lot to answer for. Utter vandalism! Someone could have been killed.'

Douglas clicked his tongue. 'And talking of someone being killed,' he whispered back, 'did you see the look that lad gave me? He looked as if he might have liked to have a go at me.'

Wallace shrugged. 'Maybe he didn't like the way you were ogling his lass?'

Douglas pursed his lips. 'Aye, she's a looker all right. The sort who might be worth dying for.'

3

I

Tam MacOnachie was in his element. As soon as Wallace Drummond had radioed him to say that he had picked up three kayakers, one of whom had holed their kayak, he had relaxed. The important thing was that no one had drowned. That was every harbour master's worst nightmare.

An inevitable crowd had started to gather as news spread round Kyleshiffin that a rescue operation was underway. Tam had immediately put up an exclusion tape around the Drummond brothers' berth to keep the crowd back in case there was a need to give emergency treatment on the harbour.

'Here, Tam, what's this barrier thing for?' Calum Steele asked. 'You can't seriously be wanting to stop the *West Uist Chronicle* from reporting the news.'

Tam MacOnachie raised his eyes heavenwards in mock exasperation. 'Come away in then, Calum, but just promise me that you won't get in the way.'

Calum grinned and raised the tape for

Cora. 'I don't think that you have met my girlfriend — er — my assistant, Cora Melville, have you, Tam?'

Tam's face creased into the semblance of a rare smile and he shook her hand. 'No, but I ken all about you, Cora. Has no one warned you to be careful of our local newspaperman?'

Cora giggled. 'I like a bit of danger, Tam. And life with Calum is always exciting.'

'Exciting?' Tam echoed in disbelief. 'Calum Steele is exciting? Why that is the first time that I ever heard — '

But his words died on his lips as the noise of the Drummond brothers' fishing boat approached the harbour. The crowd started to cheer spontaneously.

Some minutes later Tam helped the twins tie up their boat, then lent a hand to assist the three people down.

Inspector Torquil McKinnon and Sergeant Morag Driscoll edged their way through the crowd to meet them. Crusoe was scampering at Torquil's feet, wagging his tail furiously as if he sensed that something exciting was happening.

'Well done, lads,' Torquil said, slipping an arm about Wallace's shoulders.

'You'll be letting us have an official report, won't you, Wallace?' said Morag, with her

43

tongue in her cheek. She was well aware of the twins' dislike of paperwork.

'Aye, Sergeant Driscoll, we will that,' Wallace replied with a rueful grin. 'As soon as I can get my brother to stop drooling over the damsel he just rescued.'

Torquil looked at the three people who were standing talking to Tam MacOnachie and Calum Steele, while Cora Melville stood beside Calum and scribbled away in a reporter's spiral notebook. The girl was standing with an emergency foil blanket about her shoulders. She seemed to be answering most of the questions, while one of the men, the younger of the two, who had a port-wine birthmark that extended from the right side of his forehead around his right eye, seemed to be deliberately positioning himself between her and Douglas Drummond. The other, older man stood nodding his head to confirm the girl's account.

Cora had looked up and seen Torquil and Morag. She smiled then tugged at Calum's sleeve and whispered in his ear. He turned and immediately hailed Torquil.

'Ah, Inspector McKinnon!' he called, signalling him over. 'This is Miss Rosie Barton, the writer. And this is her co-author, Jerome Morton and their agent, Henry Dodds. Miss Barton here was telling us how Douglas and his brother rescued them out at the Cruadalach Isles. From what I hear it was you who set the rescue in motion with the pipes.'

Torquil held the tape up and let Morag through before joining them himself. Crusoe yapped twice and scampered along at his feet. He saw Rosie Barton in her silvery emergency blanket and headed straight for her, his tail wagging furiously.

'That is correct, Calum. Crusoe and I were out at St Ninian's Cave doing a bit of practising and he saw them.'

'Your dog saw us?' Rosie Barton squealed with pleasure, squatting down and making a fuss over Crusoe. 'What a wonderful wee friend you have.'

'And what a great story it makes,' Calum said. 'Great human interest.'

'Don't you mean canine interest, Calum?' said Douglas with a grin.

'Aye, even better. Crusoe spots the three of you in trouble and alerts Torquil. He lets you know that help is on its way and then . . . '

'Then this wonderful man rescued us,' said Rosie, standing and smiling up at Douglas Drummond.

'Aye! Aye!' exclaimed Calum gleefully. 'We'll need a photograph of you all. I'm going to write it all up and it will be front page of the *Chronicle*, but more than that, I'll get it on the Scottish TV news at six tonight. Cora, get your camera.'

Jerome Morton took a pace forward and held out a restraining hand towards Cora. 'No pictures!' he snapped. 'And that's enough of an interview. We don't really want any publicity.'

II

Lachlan sat in the front of the old Morris J-type van that Murdoch Jamieson had driven and kept on the road for decades. With the star-map picture emblazoned on its sides and the *Heavens Above* logo of his show, the van which was universally known as the Star Wagon was pretty much a star in its own right. Viewers regularly saw Murdoch driving to some location where he would slide back the roof panel to allow his five-inch refractor telescope to peep out in readiness to scan whatever heavenly object was the subject of the latest programme.

Despite only having one eye, Murdoch drove like a rally driver, flinging the Star Wagon around corners and causing Gavin McIntyre in the back to hurtle from side to side, desperately clutching his cameras and equipment.

'Murdoch, let's just get there in one piece!'

Gavin cried after the Star Wagon crossed a hump and he bumped his head on the roof.

'Oh, hold your wheesht!' Murdoch rebuked him. 'It is for you and the news story that we are travelling so fast.'

'I am praying for us all,' said Lachlan with a rueful smile.

Murdoch turned into Kyleshiffin and coasted into a parking spot alongside the harbour wall. 'Your prayers were answered then, Lachlan. We're here.'

Gavin opened the rear door and jumped out. He ran towards the crowd and the others followed.

'Excuse me, excuse me! Scottish TV News!' Gavin called out, edging his way through the crowd.

The crowd parted willingly and someone raised the tape for him to duck under. With the skill of a seasoned professional Gavin hoisted his camera in readiness and introduced himself to the group at the centre.

Jerome Morton stuck his chin out belligerently and shook his head. He jerked his thumb backwards in Calum Steele's direction. 'I've just told this guy that we don't want any pictures or any publicity.'

'But this is news, Mr Morton,' Calum protested. 'The Kyleshiffin public have a right to know about a daring rescue here in the waters around West Uist.' And then he held out a territorial arm and glared at Gavin. 'And when I say that it is news, it is a *West Uist Chronicle* news story, not Scottish TV!'

'And I said — no pictures!' Jerome Morton persisted.

'Oh stop it, Jerome,' Rosie Barton said. 'Of course it is news. We were rescued from what could have been an awful situation and we have no right to stop the news process.'

'I agree with Rosie,' said Henry Dodds, the older man. 'What has got into you, Jerome? This is the first time that I've ever known you shun free publicity. Don't you want to sell your book?'

'That's more like it,' said Gavin, raising his camera and ignoring Calum. 'Could you just tell us a little about the rescue and I'll film.'

'Well, we are all on a kayaking holiday. Jerome and I are writers and Henry is our agent. We crossed from North Uist and were planning to come for Dr Horne's lectures about the Grand Cross. Well — '

She stopped suddenly, staring past Gavin's camera. Her eyes opened wide and her lips curled in disgust. 'You!' she exclaimed.

Gavin swung the camera round to train it on the subject of her disdainful look. Everyone else did as well.

Lachlan and Murdoch had come under the

tape and approached.

'Hello, Rosie, long time no see,' said Murdoch.

'Hello, Murdoch,' she replied. 'But it hasn't been long enough, in my opinion.'

A muscle seemed to twitch in Murdoch Jamieson's jaw, as if he had suddenly clenched his teeth.

Gavin switched off his camera and lowered it. He looked from one to the other in amazement.

'This maybe is not the best time or place for our reunion,' Murdoch replied, his media-ready smile back in place. 'I had no intention of intruding on your news bulletin, Gavin. Please proceed.'

'I wouldn't believe that for a moment,' came a voice from behind them.

Calum nudged Cora and whispered to her. 'I hope you are getting pictures of this, lassie.'

She winked and nodded at her iPhone and the video that she was recording.

'Excellent, Cora. I think . . . ' Calum began, then he realized that there was further drama unfolding. The voice that had just chirped in belonged to Dr Janet Horne, the astrologer that they had met shortly before in the *Chronicle* offices. She was accompanied by the unmistakable figure of Dr Melissa Mathieson.

'I heard that you were coming to do an episode of your show, Murdoch,' said Dr Horne. 'And of course, here you are just when there is a bit of news and a camera.'

'This is Gavin — my cameraman!' returned Murdoch.

Dr Horne laughed. 'Exactly my point! An astronomer and an astronomical ego that needs to have every moment of its life filmed.'

Melissa Mathieson touched her arm. The two women in their flamboyant clothes seemed so incongruous on a harbour beside a fishing boat. She pointed to the trio of rescued people.

'Aren't we forgetting the point, actually?' Melissa said. 'There is news to be told. These poor people have had an accident. It seems to me this is proof about the Grand Cross that is coming.' She took a deep breath, her expression one almost of fear. Then she added, 'Cosmic forces are at work. It has begun and the world needs to be aware of it!'

III

Ewan had brewed a huge pot of tea in readiness for the morning meeting and was keen to hear about the rescue.

Morag, Torquil and Wallace sat down in the

various easy chairs in the rest room and watched as Ewan laid the tea tray on the ping-pong table and poured each of them a mug of his strong tea. He turned as the microwave pinged and took out a plate with the steaming transit pasties that Morag had brought in. He divided them into halves and arranged them in a neat circle on the plate.

'Where is Douglas?' he asked.

Wallace raised his eyes ceiling wards. 'My dear brother is in love, I am thinking.'

'In love?'

'It seems so,' said Morag, taking her tea and reaching for one of the pasties. 'That Rosie Barton that he rescued . . . '

Wallace cleared his throat. 'That *we* rescued!' he corrected.

'Aye, that the pair of you rescued, thanks to Torquil having spotted them.' She winked at her boss then went on, 'Anyway, she is a writer and a real good-looker.'

'What does she write?' Ewan asked.

'Paranormal stuff. She and her friend Jerome Morton have co-authored a string of bestsellers about ghosts, ghouls and haunted places. They say they came to hear Dr Horne's lectures about all these planetary goings-on.'

Torquil reached down and stroked Crusoe, who had curled up at his feet. 'And then

Melissa Mathieson, the candle shop lady, came along with that Dr Horne and started telling everyone about some sort of planetary configuration that she said is of some significance. I suspect it may have been a ploy to get people to go to the lecture tonight.'

Morag nodded. 'Yes, she seems to think that the kayakers' accident was a result of this heavenly influence. And, that it was just the start of things.'

Torquil shook his head. 'Actually, I think it is a lot of nonsense. After they had all gone Lachlan told me that his pal Murdoch Jamieson says astronomical events always bring out what Murdoch calls the loony brigade. Apparently he has no truck with astrology.'

'That was clear enough,' agreed Wallace. 'But none of them seems to have much time for Murdoch Jamieson. I thought there was going to be some sort of a fight between that Rosie Barton, Dr Horne and him.'

'Aye, it looks like they have had dealings before,' Torquil replied. And he told Ewan about the encounter.

'So eventually, Murdoch's cameraman, Gavin, persuaded them to have some video film taken about the rescue. I guess they must be happy about it, because they got a free plug for the lecture tonight. Murdoch

Jamieson said that he was going to go along too, so perhaps there will be stars flying after all.'

They all laughed at that.

Suddenly, there was a crash behind them and they all looked round to see the teapot smashed on the floor.

'Oh, Ewan, you must have put it down on the edge of the table,' Morag said, jumping up to get a mop from the broom cupboard.

'I put it in the middle of the table,' Ewan replied. His normally ruddy face had suddenly gone pale. 'You don't think . . . ?'

Wallace tossed back his head and guffawed. 'Och, get your feet back on the ground, Ewan my man. All this talk of astrology mumbo-jumbo has just freaked you out. I say we go along to this meeting tonight and hear what the heebie-jeebie starry folk are on about.' He shook his head. 'If that Rosie Barton lassie is going then I expect my brother will be trailing along in her wake. I'd better be there to watch over him.'

IV

The Duncan Institute was packed to capacity that evening. Doctor Mathieson had intro-duced Dr Horne, who took to the podium of the old stage and was greeted with rapturous applause by a strong contingent of astrology enthusiasts. There was mere polite acknowledgement from a smaller part of the audience, which included Murdoch Jamieson, Gavin McIntyre and Lachlan.

'You see,' Torquil whispered to Morag — they were sitting with Ewan and Wallace Drummond in the back row. 'It looks as if there really are two factions here.'

'Aye,' Wallace agreed. 'And it looks as if Douglas has aligned himself with that Rosie Barton's clique.' He nodded his head at the front row on the other side of the hall where Douglas was sitting beside Rosie Barton and her two colleagues. It was apparent from their body language that there was chemistry at work between them. It was equally apparent from Jerome Morton's frequent glances at them that he had quite other feelings about Douglas.

Torquil smiled. The twins, who were so alike in many ways, had always had different tastes in women. Rosie Barton, with her slim build, pretty, freckled face and blonde hair was exactly Douglas's type.

His eye strayed to the other people sitting on the front row. One was Henry Dodds, Rosie Barton and Jerome Morton's agent, and the other was Dr Melissa Mathieson, who had taken the seat at the end of the row after introducing Dr Horne. Henry Dodds kept flashing glances at Dr Mathieson. It looked as if he, too, was well and truly smitten.

'Ladies and gentlemen, welcome,' began Dr Horne. 'It is gratifying to find so many fellow seekers after the truth gathered here tonight on what is the brink of a huge revelation.' She smiled at Rosie Barton and Jerome Morton. 'I see that we have some celebrated writers among us, so welcome to them.' And to emphasize their presence she nodded her head and clapped her hands encouragingly. Most of the rest of the audience followed suit.

'She didn't mean us, then!' Calum Steele whispered aside to Cora with a wry grin. 'That's a bad move on her part. You always need to get the local press on your side.'

Cora was conscious that her boyfriend was still cross about Dr Horne calling him a 'little man'. 'Does that mean you are going to give her a bad press, Calum?'

'Goodness me, no, Cora. We are journalists and we are here to report. Let's just hope that things warm up a bit, like they seemed to do on the harbour this afternoon.'

Doctor Horne continued, 'And, of course, it is good to see that we also have a strong group of astronomers here, including the famous host of *Heavens Above*, Murdoch Jamieson.' She smiled at him, although the smile seemed to have little warmth. She clapped before he had any chance to come back at her and the audience applauded politely.

'Perhaps this event can act as a sort of bridgehead between astrology and astronomy. Or rather, act as a return to our shared ancestry. As you all know, astrology and astronomy were once one science, once a single art.'

A few sniggers and snorts of derision came from the astronomy contingent.

Doctor Horne ignored it and began slowly walking across the stage with the auto-control for her powerpoint projector in her hand. 'I want to show you a few slides to put things into perspective. Firstly, here is a schematic of the solar system.'

The room darkened and an image flashed up on the screen with the sun surrounded by the planets. The planets slowly started to move.

'The first phenomenon that we are all interested in is the transit of Mercury across the sun. If you watch, you will see that as we speed up the planetary orbits the planet Mercury appears to cross between the Earth and the sun. This is what we will see at sunrise and for a few hours after.'

She put up another video clip, which showed a small black dot pass across the sun.

She smiled at the audience. 'Transits of Mercury occur several times in a century. Transits of its neighbouring planet, Venus, are much rarer. We had one in 2004 and there will be another in 2012, but there won't be another for a hundred and five years. On this occasion Mercury will be close to Venus in astrological terms, so in a sense they will kiss.'

Murdoch Jamieson gave a loud snort of derision. 'They are, if you think forty million kilometres is close.'

She smiled at her heckler. 'I said in *astrological* terms. They will be close enough to exert a combined effect. They will be conjunct in Aquarius with Jupiter and Uranus. Indeed, their effect is starting to make itself felt.'

Melissa Mathieson nodded her head. 'Just as I said it would,' she enthused. 'And we have already seen its effect today,' she added, turning and smiling at the three rescued kayakers along from her.

Henry Dodds leaned towards her and tapped the back of her hand. 'That is absolutely fascinating,' he whispered to her. 'I would like to chat with you about this later.'

Doctor Mathieson's cheeks coloured slightly and she smiled back, but said nothing.

'But all of this is merely a prelude,' went on Dr Horne. 'The transit of Mercury is rather like the touch-paper of a great firework. Think of Mercury as the messenger of the gods, the torch-bearer. The fact is that far more powerful phenomena are about to take place as the great planets take up their positions in the zodiac. Jupiter will be in conjunction with Uranus, both will be opposite Saturn and Venus will be opposite Pluto. If we chart this properly you will see that it gives us a definite Grand Cross.'

She brought up a slide showing an astrological chart with the planets labelled accordingly. Quite distinctly, lines appeared, showing the shape of a cross. Dr Horne smiled. 'The last time this happened was in July 1692.'

She waited and flashed up another slide. It was of women clad in puritan dress. Then slowly another image formed in the background. It was a hangman's noose.

'In case you are not aware,' she continued, 'that heralded the start of the Salem witch trials in America.'

The news was met by silence at first, then by several sighs and intakes of breath from the astrology contingent. Then by a belly laugh from Murdoch Jamieson. It was quickly followed by a cacophony of guffaws and murmurs of ridicule from the astronomy supporters gathered about him.

At the back of the hall Torquil noted his uncle, Lachlan McKinnon, bending his head as if feeling intensely embarrassed to be in the middle of one faction.

'Utter twaddle and balderdash!' cried Murdoch. 'You would think that we were still living in the Euphrates Basin several centuries before the birth of Christ.'

Lachlan's head shot up and he patted Murdoch on the arm as if to tell him to calm down.

Murdoch glanced at the Padre and laughed. 'That may have been a slip of the tongue on my part,' he explained. 'I did not mean that I accept the birth of Jesus Christ as being in any way divine, as my old friend the Reverend McKinnon here would like to believe. No, the birth of the said person merely gives us a convenient way of measuring time. But what I meant to say was that this nonsense about planetary positions is simple superstition. It has no academic credibility at all.'

Calum Steele was scribbling away furiously. 'I love it, Cora. I love it,' he whispered. 'This is just what we wanted.'

Cora was busily studying her iPhone, scrolling through the Google entries for the Salem witch trials.

Suddenly Rosie Barton stood up. 'Academic credibility? That's rich coming from a man who has made a career out of stealing his researchers' work.'

She stood staring at him, daring him to retort.

Instead, with a rueful laugh and a shake of the head he stood up and made his way from the hall.

The whole audience sat in stunned silence for a few moments, then one by one the astronomy supporters started to filter out. Rosie Barton sat down again.

'As I said,' Dr Horne went on, 'the Grand Cross has probably started to manifest itself. It presages doom, destruction, deceit and — exposure!'

V

The Bonnie Prince Charlie Tavern was heaving when Torquil, Calum and Cora arrived in the vanguard of many of the audience who had gone straight there from the Duncan Institute. Doctors Horne and Mathieson and several enthusiastic astrologers were sitting at one table drinking cocktails while Murdoch Jamieson and Gavin McIntyre were standing with a group of astronomers at one end of the bar, sipping pints.

'What will you have, Calum?' Torquil asked.

'A pint of Heather Ale and a chaser for me.'

'An orange juice, thank you, Torquil.'

'We'll meet you back at the bar in a few minutes,' Calum said conspiratorially. 'We just need to do a bit of eavesdropping. Cora, you take the women and I'll position myself to hear the blokes.'

Torquil grinned and made his way to the bar. Mollie McFadden, the doughty landlady of almost sixty years, was pulling a pint with well-practised ease as she marshalled her staff as they bustled about catering for the sudden influx of customers. She peered at Torquil through her pebble-thick spectacles and gave him a broad smile. 'Is the Padre not coming in tonight?'

Torquil shook his head. 'No, I think he had enough excitement at the lecture.'

'Ah, I heard all about it. It seemed to have been a lively affair. It looks as though the bar is divided into two camps.' She finished serving one customer and took his order.

As she pulled a pint she nodded at the large plasma-screen television. 'The six o'clock news on Scottish TV had a piece about the kayak rescue. All in all it has been a pretty exciting day in Kyleshiffin. The Drummond boys came out of it like heroes.'

Torquil grinned as the door opened and Morag and Wallace Drummond came in. 'And speaking of the devil, you had better add another pint and a half, Mollie.'

A few moments later the three of them were clinking glasses and chatting about the lecture.

'Where is Douglas?' Torquil asked, with a thin smile.

'I think you know very well where he is, Torquil McKinnon,' Wallace returned. 'He's doing his puppy-dog trick and trying to inveigle himself into the affections of Miss Rosie Barton. They were all ambling along behind us and I wouldn't be surprised — '

The door squeaked open and Douglas held it open for Rosie Barton, Jerome Morton and Henry Dodds. Douglas waved to them before steering a course through to the snug where there was often a free table.

'See what I mean?' said Wallace. 'Besotted.'

Morag and Torquil exchanged amused glances.

A moment later, Dodds came out of the snug and began weaving his way through the crowd to the bar. Torquil gestured with his glass in his direction as he strayed towards Dr Horne's table. 'I'm willing to bet that he's another one who's got it bad.'

'What do you mean, Torquil?'

'He means he looks as if he's fallen in love with someone,' put in Morag.

'Aye, well, it may be love in his case,' Wallace remarked, taking a hefty gulp of beer. He lowered his glass and wiped foam from his upper lip. 'In Douglas's case I bet it is at least sixty-per-cent lust.'

VI

Ewan McPhee had risen just after dawn and set off early. His plan was to go up on the moor above Kyleshiffin to practise his hammer before opening the station. Although he was earlier than usual he knew that many of the shopkeepers on Harbour Street would already be opening their shops in readiness for the day's business.

As usual he had to endure the banter of the likes of Willie Staig and Gordon Allardyce.

Then, at the end of the street he saw Eggy MacOnachie walking from the chandlery towards the harbour wall. He saw him stagger backwards, then start forward and steady himself on the harbour wall.

'Goodness, is Tam MacOnachie ill? Is he having a heart attack?' Ewan mumbled to himself, as he opened the throttle on the moped for all it was worth.

Tam MacOnachie heard Nippy's engine noise and looked round. Then, seeing Ewan, he began gesticulating wildly. 'PC McPhee! Come quick.'

A few moments later Ewan skidded to a halt.

'L — Look!' the chandler gasped, pointing wildly to the water beyond and well below the harbour wall.

Ewan jumped off Nippy, kicked the stand down and ran over.

A woman's body was floating face down in Kyleshiffin harbour.

4

I

The Padre had been up at daybreak to take Crusoe for a walk and play two holes on his way to St Ninian's Church.

After going in and saying his prayers silently he opened the door to the tower and mounted the steps. As he approached the top he heard Murdoch talking in what was clearly his television voice. Accordingly, rather than loudly hailing him he advanced up the last few steps as quietly as he could. Sure enough, he found Murdoch pointing to a laptop screen that was wired up to a large telescope. Gavin McIntyre was filming him.

'And there you see the solar disc with this tiny wee dot gradually making its way across it. It is a quite remarkable phenomenon that really makes one realize how small, how insignificant we human beings are in the scheme of things. That wee dot is the planet Mercury, the closest planet to the sun.'

He stood up and Gavin followed him, zooming in on a shoulder-and-head shot.

'We will be charting the transit and later on

in the programme we will be able to show you the conjunction of Jupiter and Uranus.'

He gave a short laugh. 'In a way it is not surprising that in the past people have thought that these heavenly bodies were gods and that they had a bearing on our feeble lives here on earth. In fact, last night I attended a lecture right here on West Uist when the celebrity astrologer Dr Janet Horne actually told the audience that a particular arrangement of the planets was about to bring down some sort of catastrophic event.'

He smiled at the camera and then glanced over his shoulder at the sun. 'Well, so far so good. It is a bright morning; we can see both the sun and Mercury. No catastrophe has happened as yet.' His smile curved into a smirk. 'Maybe, just maybe, there is nothing in the pseudo-science of astrology.' And with a wink of his good eye at the camera he stood and waited for Gavin to stop filming.

'Lachlan! Good morning,' he said at last. 'I am surprised that you did not get up earlier to watch the start of the transit.'

'Ah, a fascinating thing it is, too, but I had other things to attend to first. Like Crusoe, our wee dog, who is waiting patiently outside the church door, a couple of holes and, of course, my morning conversation with the Lord.'

Gavin grinned. 'I wouldn't get him started on that if I was you, Padre. The old boy is such a heathen.'

'I know that, Gavin. And I heard that he couldn't resist having a jibe at Dr Horne's lecture last night.'

'Well, all that hocus-pocus annoys me,' Murdoch returned. 'This is the twenty-first century, Lachlan. I am a scientist and it is my duty to present hard facts to my viewers. All that twaddle about a Grand Cross, witches and what-not, can only alarm folk who are gullible enough to think that planets and stars actually impinge on their lives. How ridiculous to think that those great bodies millions and millions of miles away can affect people here on earth according to the positions that appertained at the moment they were born. It . . . it defies logic and common sense.'

The noise of a motorbike engine being kicked into life came from the direction of the manse. A moment later they saw Torquil hurtling down the road on his Bullet.

Crusoe saw him too, and started barking down below.

'Hmm, there must be an emergency of some sort,' Lachlan mused. 'Torquil doesn't usually leave Crusoe behind like that. And he won't even have had his breakfast.'

II

Torquil arrived at the harbour just after Morag. Calum and Cora were already there, staring down at the body of a woman who was being examined by Dr Ralph McLelland, the local GP and police surgeon.

Ewan was sitting on the harbour wall, a blanket round his broad shoulders, sipping a mug of tea.

Tam MacOnachie met them and explained. 'Ewan McPhee dived in and fished her out. He's a hero.'

'Not at all! I am no such thing, Tam,' Ewan said, pushing himself off the wall and coming to meet his superior officers. 'I fear that she was long past help.'

Ralph McLelland removed his stethoscope and stood up. He was one of Torquil's oldest friends along with Calum Steele. The three of them had thought themselves to be like the Three Musketeers when they were attending the Kyleshiffin School under Miss Bella Melville's watchful eye. Then they had grown up and gone their separate ways; Torquil to study law at university before becoming a police officer, Calum to throw himself into journalism, and Ralph to study medicine.

After graduating from Glasgow University, Ralph had fully intended becoming a pathologist and had studied forensic medicine and medical jurisprudence, until his uncle had died suddenly. Family loyalty had then overcome personal academic ambition and he returned to West Uist to take over the old boy's medical practice, as well as his post as honorary police surgeon to the West Uist branch of the Hebridean Constabulary. On several occasions in the past his forensic skills had come in very handy.

He had obviously reacted to an emergency call and was still wearing his pyjamas under a West Uist tweed jacket. 'Not such a good start to the day, Torquil,' he said. 'I am afraid that the lady seems to have been dead for a few hours. I am guessing you'll be wanting to have a post-mortem?'

Torquil winced as he looked down at the body of Dr Horne. Her face was as white and lifeless as the underbelly of a dead fish.

'Did she drown?' he asked.

'Looks like it.'

'Could she have tripped and fallen in somehow?' Morag queried.

Torquil looked doubtful. 'And fallen over this wall? She would have to be pretty drunk to do that, I think.'

'But that doesn't explain the bump and the injury on the back of her head,' Ralph said. 'I'll be able to tell you more when I get her on the mortuary table.'

'Knocked from behind?' Torquil said, bending down to look at the body. She was dressed exactly as he remembered from the previous evening, with her bangles hanging forlornly on her mottled wrists. 'That puts an entirely different complexion on things.'

Calum coughed and sidled closer, his spiral notebook at the ready. 'Are we talking murder here?'

'No comment as yet, Calum,' Torquil replied as he stood up.

He looked beyond him and walked over to the harbour wall. 'Have you seen these markings before, Tam?' he asked, pointing to a couple of wavy chalked lines on the harbour wall, beside a huge pile of creels and green fishing nets.

'Nothing. They weren't there yesterday. Kids, I imagine. They look like waves to me.'

'I'm not so sure it is kids, but I agree they look like waves,' Torquil said. 'If I am not mistaken that's the astrological sign for Aquarius, the water-carrier.'

Calum opened his notebook and started jotting notes. 'We'll have a picture of that on your clicky box Cora, please. Then we had better get back to the *Chronicle* office. We have a story to run.'

Decorum stopped him from smiling at the

thought of the scoop he planned to write. Sensitivity was not one of his strong suits.

III

Lachlan was still up the church tower with Murdoch and Gavin when Torquil phoned him to explain his sudden departure and to request that he look after Crusoe.

'In the harbour?' Lachlan exclaimed. 'That's terrible. And it looks suspicious, you say?'

Murdoch and Gavin stared at him as they watched him talking on his mobile phone to his nephew.

'Of course I will look after him. He saw you go and he barked a bit. I think he must have missed his trip on the Bullet. Don't worry, I'll go and see to him now. He's waiting patiently at the church door.'

'Bad news?' Murdoch asked, as Lachlan stowed the phone away in a side pocket.

Lachlan began filling his pipe. 'An unbeliev-able tragedy,' he replied. 'Ewan McPhee pulled a woman's body out of Kyleshiffin harbour. That was the emergency Torquil went off on.'

'And is she OK?' Murdoch queried.

'Dead, I am afraid. And they think it looks

suspicious. She had a bang on the back of her head. It is possible she could have been bludgeoned.'

'Is it someone local, Padre?' Gavin asked.

Lachlan tamped the tobacco down in the bowl of his pipe and flicked his lighter into flame. 'It was Dr Janet Horne.'

Both Murdoch and Gavin stared at him in horror.

'Streuth!' Gavin exclaimed, incredulously. 'Maybe the old bird was onto something after all, what with all her talk about planetary arrangements and disaster.'

Lachlan puffed his pipe into life. 'Who knows? The universe is a mysterious place, as we all know.'

Murdoch snorted disdainfully. 'Not that mysterious, Lachlan,' he said, his face visibly paler than a few moments before. 'She and I had our differences, but I would say that there was nothing predictable about her death.'

IV

After phoning his uncle, Torquil had gone to his office and put a call through to Superintendent Lumsden, his superior officer at his office on Benbecula. It was never a task that he relished, for they had history. To Torquil's slight relief he was not in the office yet, the phone having been answered by Torquil's fiancée, Sergeant Lorna Golspie. He told her about the discovery of Dr Horne's body.

'Goodness me! How awful. And is Ewan all right?' she asked concernedly. 'That would be a shock to anyone, but we know how sensitive he is, for all his great size and strength.'

Torquil grinned. 'He's a bit shaken up and a bit embarrassed at all the attention he has received, diving into the harbour like that, but he will survive. The poor lad always seems to be finding bodies.'

'You'll have to be careful yourself, darling. You know how Superintendent Lumsden keeps looking for ways to get at you.'

'Aye, my love. He holds me responsible for the time he was suspended.'

Lorna sighed. 'He would like nothing better than to split us up.'

Torquil felt his hackles rise. Superintendent Lumsden had originally sent Lorna to the island to do an efficiency study on the way Torquil ran the West Uist branch of the Hebridean Constabulary. He had expected her to report a mountain of inefficiency, but instead they had solved a murder case together and fallen in love.

'Nothing will split us up, darling,' he reassured her. 'And don't worry, you know that 'careful' is my middle name.'

After he finished his call he went through to the rest room where Morag was fussing over Ewan, ensuring that he was adequately dried off, warmed up with a blanket around his shoulders and supplied with hot sweet tea. As an additional precaution against him catching a chill she had added a medicinal teaspoon of Glen Corlan whisky.

'What did Superintendent Lumsden say?' Morag asked.

'He wasn't in. Lorna is going to fill him in when he arrives. For the moment we can't do anything other than record that the death of Dr Horne seems suspicious. When did Ralph McLelland say he'd be doing the post-mortem?'

'At eleven o'clock, after his morning surgery.'

Ewan gulped a mouthful of tea. 'Do — do you want me to attend it, boss?'

Torquil shook his head with a wry smile. Lorna's words about Ewan's sensitivity rang in his ears. A post-mortem was no place for someone of a squeamish disposition.

'No, Ewan, I'll be going to this one. You've done your duty already.' He glanced at his watch. 'But it is still early and I for one

74

haven't had breakfast yet. What say we ring Gordon Allardyce and order some of his transit pasties?'

Morag shook her head. 'I'll order them for you, boys, but I'm not going to have one two days in a row.'

'Actually, boss,' Ewan said. 'I think I've gone off the planetary stuff. I think I'd rather have a bacon roll if you don't mind.'

That settled it for Morag. The prospect of a bacon roll was too much. 'OK, I'm in for one of those as well.'

And she and Ewan winked at each other.

V

It was after nine o'clock by the time Rosie Barton came down to breakfast in the Masonic Arms Hotel dining room. Henry Dodds had arrived five minutes before and was sitting at a table in the bay window, buttering toast while he waited for his bacon and eggs to arrive. Rosie had only just sat down opposite him when Jerome Morton came in, yawning, as he ran his fingers through his hair as if to comb it into some semblance of tidiness.

'And where did you two get to last night, if a mere agent may ask?' Henry said with forced joviality.

Jerome eyed him askance then replied sourly. 'The expression, I believe, is something like 'cats on the tiles'. It seems that Rosie has a new boyfriend.'

Rosie's lips curved into a humourless smile. 'Funny how new is always preferable to old,' she said pointedly.

'Then maybe I should try something new — and younger!' Jerome countered.

Henry raised his hands, placatingly. 'Children, please! Can't we agree to get on until this business is all over? We need to work together.'

Jerome sat back and scowled at them both. He began drumming his fingers on the table. Then, after a few moments, said, 'The service in this dive is hopeless.' He raised his palms upwards and pointedly looked round at the otherwise deserted dining room. 'I mean, I guess that we are the last of the guests to come down, but it looks like they've forgotten us.'

'Relax, Jerome,' Rosie said, as she took one of Henry's pieces of toast and started to scrape a thin layer of butter over it. 'We aren't in any great hurry, are we? The chandler said it would take a few days before my kayak is repaired properly and seaworthy again.'

'I know, but . . . '

The swing doors from the kitchen opened

and a pretty sixteen-year-old girl with red hair and freckles entered. She was dressed in a black dress with a white apron and was carrying a plate of bacon and eggs and a pitcher of milk.

With a tremulous smile she served Henry, then pulled out a notepad and pencil from her apron pocket. 'G-Good morning. I'm Katrina MacFarlane. My dad owns the hotel and we are very . . . very pleased to have you staying with us.'

'Why's that, Katrina?' Jerome asked without a trace of a smile.

Katrina blushed. 'Well . . . well, it is nice to have famous people staying.'

'Famous, are we, Katrina? What for? I don't think we're famous.'

Katrina's blush seemed to spread down her neck. 'You are writers, aren't you? I mean, my dad said you are.' She coughed as she prepared to slip into automatic hotel-speak. 'Are you ready to give me your breakfast order?'

'Just tea and a small kipper for me, please,' Rosie said with a smile. 'And yes, we are writers, but we're not really famous, Katrina.'

Jerome glared at Rosie and snatched the menu from the table and began deliberating.

'It's terrible news, isn't it?' Katrina said, gaining confidence from Rosie's demeanour.

'I must say it made me feel sick when I heard about it. I don't think I could eat breakfast if I were you.'

Jerome laid the menu down on the table and leaned forward. 'What are you garbling on about?' he snapped. 'Aren't you supposed to be encouraging your guests to eat? Shouldn't you be telling us what a finely cooked breakfast your gourmet chef is preparing for us, and not telling us that you couldn't eat breakfast?'

Katrina's lower lip began to tremble and tears seemed to form in her eyes.

Rosie stood up and put a comforting arm about Katrina's shoulders, 'Jerome Morton, you are a brute and boor. How dare you be so rude to Katrina!' She gave the young waitress a reassuring one-armed hug. 'What's the matter, sweetheart? What terrible news are you talking about?'

'You . . . you . . . you mean you haven't heard? It is all round Kyleshiffin.'

'For goodness sake,' said Jerome, impatiently. 'What is all round Kyleshiffin?'

'D-D-Doctor Horne, your friend. She was found drowned in the harbour this morning!' And with that it seemed that she could no longer hold back the tears. She let out a gasp then began sobbing uncontrollably. She broke free from Rosie's comforting arm and ran for the safety of the kitchen, leaving three stunned guests staring after her.

VI

Melissa Mathieson always rose at sunrise when the sun's influence was most profound after the long hours of darkness. Every other morning she would go swimming from Heulich Bay, rejoicing in sharing the waters with the myriads of creatures who led their lives in the sea. As one born under the sign of Cancer, the crab, she felt an affinity with them. But this morning was one of her early-morning work days. And again, she found the ether to be clearest and her diagnostic and curative skills were at their sharpest in the hours after sunrise.

She spent an hour working on hair samples that clients had sent her, so that she could do an analysis of their problems, be they physical, psychological or personal. Then she would meditate on each and send messages to the angels to help them. Where she thought it appropriate she would make up crystal or herbal essences for them, which she would send by the first post.

After a frugal breakfast of figs and green tea she dressed herself and prepared to open her shop, Crystals and Candles. She felt energized after her healing work and ready to take on whatever the world threw at her.

Within moments of opening up, three of her friends came in, all of them pale-faced and agitated.

'Melissa! Have you any more news about the tragedy?' asked a middle-aged woman dressed in black from head to toe.

'It is so frightening. I think she may have had an idea it was going to happen to her,' said a younger woman dressed in a thin, flowery dress with a scarlet bandanna tied around her head. She looked like a beautiful gypsy girl.

'I am just so shocked,' agreed another young woman dressed in Goth clothes with a pierced nose and multiple earrings. 'And I know it is an awful thing to say, but she has been a sort of martyr. This is proof, a vindication of astrology. She virtually told everyone that it was going to happen.'

Melissa raised her hands for silence. 'Ladies, please. What are you talking about?'

The older woman's jaw dropped. 'Good heavens! You mean that you haven't heard all the consternation and the comings and goings?'

Melissa shook her head, feeling her heart quicken its beat. Their agitation had infected her. 'I was busy. Working!'

'Doctor Horne drowned in the harbour!' the woman announced. 'Heaven take her soul.'

VII

A bacon roll washed down with a couple more mugs of strong tea, this time without Morag's medicinal whisky, had restored Ewan to his usual equanimity. He had returned to the station desk ready for action.

He had not expected his first customer to be Ming McDonald. He was dressed as usual in his waterproofs and baseball hat, with the inevitable unlit cigar clenched between his teeth.

'Ah! PC McPhee! I have a complaint to make,' he said, as soon as he entered the station, almost before the tinkle of the door-bell had gone. 'I heard about that poor woman that you dragged out of the harbour this morning. That was brave of you and highly commendable, by the way.'

'Oh jings! It was n — '

Ming McDonald pressed on, cutting Ewan short. 'Well, it is a disgrace, that is what it is!'

'I'm sorry, I don't — '

'A disgrace! That could have been me, you know.'

'How is that, Mr McDonald?'

Ming McDonald made the sign of the cross. 'Aye, I slipped on those harbour steps myself only yesterday morning. It was only my cat-like reflexes that saved me. I could have banged my head, knocked myself out and fallen into the harbour like that lassie. Those steps are a disgrace. All covered in slime. It is a wonder there hasn't been a fatality before now.'

Ewan eyed him askance. 'So — er — what exactly are you complaining about, Mr McDonald?'

'It is not what, but who!' Ming McDonald declared with gusto. 'I am complaining about Tam MacOnachie, the so-called harbour master. What sort of a message does he send out to the world with the state of those harbour steps? It is a disgrace.'

Ewan sighed inwardly. He knew he would have to at the very least record the complaint in the duty book. He picked up a pen in readiness.

'Right then, Mr McDonald. Tell me exactly what you want to complain about and I will make an official record of it.'

Ming McDonald stared at him in horror. 'Official? I never said that I wanted to make an official complaint. I am just exercising my right to complain to the police about the slipshod way that he looks after his harbour. I don't want you to make it official. I just want you to tick him off.'

Ewan suppressed the urge to reach across the desk and grab the unlit cigar from Ming McDonald's lips. The word 'diplomacy' flashed through his mind. Torquil was always reminding him that a good police officer had to be a paragon of diplomacy. He laid the pen down and smiled.

'Leave it with me, Mr McDonald. We will have a quiet word with him.'

Ming McDonald removed his cigar and smiled back. 'That's exactly what is needed, PC McPhee. A quiet word. No sense in anyone getting riled, is there?'

VIII

Although Torquil was sympathetic to Ewan's squeamishness, he recognized that he himself always felt a touch queasy whenever he had to attend the autopsy room at Kyleshiffin Cottage Hospital.

Ralph McLelland had been late finishing his surgery and had added to the lateness by stopping off at Gordon Allardyce's to pick up a couple of mutton pies.

'And you needn't look at me like that,

Torquil McKinnon,' he said with mock severity as he munched on a pie when he eventually arrived at the pathology wing of the hospital where Torquil had been kicking his heels. 'Don't forget I was called out early and I haven't had my breakfast yet. How is Ewan, by the way? We don't want our hammer-throwing champion to go down with pneumonia.'

'It would take more than a dip in the sea to do that to the big lad,' Torquil returned with a grin, as Ralph held the door to the pathology wing open for him. But as he watched Ralph chew his pie, he noticed a trickle of grease at the corner of his mouth that made his own stomach squirm. The smell of disinfectant was quite overpowering and, as they passed through the icy-cold refrigerator room which contained the bodies of the hospital's deceased patients until they were collected by the under-taker, or any cases awaiting postmortem examination, he felt distinctly queasy. He be-gan to wish that he had not just had a transit pastie himself.

He refused the offer of tea or coffee, but sipped a cup of iced water while he waited for Ralph to finish his pies then dress in a green surgical pyjama suit, white wellingtons and a plastic apron.

'Come on then, Torquil,' Ralph said,

pulling on a pair of rubber gloves and hauling them over the end of his sleeves. 'Conn MacVicar will have the body ready for us.'

Torquil had donned the gown and face mask that Ralph insisted everyone should wear during post-mortem examinations and followed him through to the autopsy room.

As Ralph had predicted, Conn MacVicar was busily working by the stainless-steel sink, getting the various buckets, basins and specimen containers ready.

'Hello, Inspector McKinnon,' the hospital porter-cum-mortician beamed at him. Conn was a small, tubby man with the most outrageous comb-over imaginable. 'It is good to be seeing you professionally again.'

Torquil forced a smile and willed his stomach not to betray him. 'And good to see you too, Conn.'

'A nasty business, sir,' Conn said. 'A beautiful woman like that. Tragic.'

Torquil's eye had fallen on the green sheet that covered the body on the dissecting table. A tap attached to a hose was trickling water into a gutter that ran around the edge of the table. He glanced at the extensive array of instruments laid out on a trolley in readiness for the examination and which would soon be used to cause the gutter to run with blood and other body fluids.

Ralph clapped his gloved hands together and nodded to Conn, who whipped the sheet away to reveal the naked body of Dr Janet Horne. Despite himself, Torquil felt a shiver run up his spine. The woman had obviously looked after herself and was svelte and seemed quite well muscled, like a swimmer.

'We'll start with a description of her external appearance,' Ralph said, clicking on a dictaphone.

'Examination begins at eleven-forty a.m. on 11 June . . . ' he began.

Torquil watched as he examined the head and neck, then moved around the body, describing each feature, every bruise, scar or anomaly.

' . . . but we shall see whether or not this head injury was enough to fracture the skull when we open the cranium,' Ralph dictated.

He went over the whole body. 'No signs of any bruising around the breasts or around the genitals. No sign of sexual penetration as yet. We'll take swabs.'

Once he had completed his external examinations and taken samples from under her nails and appropriate vaginal swabs, he clicked off the dictaphone and turned to Conn. 'OK, let's have a scalpel and I'll peel back the scalp.'

Torquil felt bile rise to his throat. He hated

this bit, for he knew exactly how Ralph did it. He would make an incision from behind one ear right round to behind the other. Then he would dissect the tethering tissue that held the scalp down to the skull and pull the whole scalp up over the head so that it covered the face. After that would come the circular saw to cut through the top of the skull so that it could be lifted off like a lid to expose the brain beneath.

He looked away as Ralph began his incision.

Then his mobile went off and he walked to the door and answered it.

'Really?' he said into it. 'OK, I'll go and see. Thanks. I'll see you back at the station.'

He pocketed the phone and looked over at Ralph, who was starting to work the scalp free of the cranium. 'I'm afraid I have to go, Ralph,' he said with some relief. 'Can you brief me with your results later?'

'Of course, just as soon as I have completed the examination I will let you have a preliminary report. But, as you know, it may be a while before I have an official report, especially if I need to run histology or toxicology tests.' He looked up momentarily. 'That sounded as if you might have more information?'

Torquil stood with his hand on the

doorhandle. 'It was Morag. She just took a call from Tam MacOnachie. He has found a bottle of some sort behind some creels at the harbour.'

'A bottle? What's the significance?'

'It has blood on it.'

'Ah! So it could have been a bludgeon?'

Torquil nodded. 'Exactly. But if it was, then those chalk marks may be really significant.'

'How do you mean?'

'Think about it, Ralph. It looked like the sign of Aquarius, the water-carrier. And a bottle could be a water-carrier.'

He left before Ralph started the circular saw.

5

I

Calum sat back in his editorial chair, one foot on the floor, gently pushing himself from side to side. With a mutton pie in one hand and a mug of coffee in the other, and the beautiful Cora sitting opposite him, listening to his every word, he was a happy man.

'It's going to be a cracking story, Cora. We've got the ideas for the front page pretty well sewn up. That was a great idea for a title, by the way.' He took a bite of his pie and immediately washed it down with a slurp of coffee, so fired up was he with enthusiasm that he barely chewed.

'Death in Transit! That is inspired, Cora,' he said, winking at her behind his wire-framed spectacles.

Cora gave a little shrug of her shoulders. 'It is what comes of working with you, darling. Your genius is rubbing off on me, I think.'

Calum stopped his swaying and stared at her. He blinked with embarrassment, for it was the first time she had actually called him 'darling'. For a fleeting moment his natural bachelor persona balked. The feeling was rapidly replaced by a feeling of pride. He was pleased that she thought he was a genius, and doubly proud that a girl as pretty as Cora Melville could be attracted to him. For years he had fantasized about having a relationship with Kirstie Macroon, the pretty, Scottish TV newsreader and anchor-person, yet part of him had always known that it was a relationship that was never really going to happen. It amazed him that he had held a candle for her for so long, because ever since Cora Melville had burst into his life he only had eyes for her.

But her use of the word 'darling' had flummoxed him, and he was not used to that.

'Aye!' he said simply, with a nod. He slurped more coffee then went on quickly. 'So, after we have described the finding of the body in the harbour, talked about PC Ewan McPhee's brave dive to try to rescue her, we go on to talk about her lecture last night and all that stuff about the transit and the Grand Cross.'

'And the fact that the same pattern happened during the Salem witch trials in America in 1692,' Cora added.

'Excellent!'

Cora pursed her lips and turned a page on

her notebook. 'I was just wondering, though, my darling,' she continued. 'Could we use a bit of poetic licence here?'

Calum had stopped with his pie halfway to his mouth. She had done it again. She had used the D word. He wondered whether to reciprocate, or at least follow it up with a question or two. But between thinking about it and acting upon it his mouth opened reflexively and he blurted out, 'Eh?'

Cora went on, her words tumbling out quickly as she warmed to her subject. 'Well, I just thought, the Salem witch trials are all very interesting in that they happened when there was another of these astrological Grand Cross things, but Salem was in America. It would be more interesting if there was a British connection.'

'Aye,' Calum replied, cursing himself for letting the moment go.

She held up her iPhone and pointed to it. 'I did a bit of research on the Internet with my clicky box, as you call it, and the last witch trials in this country were ten years before that, in Bideford in Devon. Three women were accused and put on trial for witchcraft. Temperance Lloyd, Mary Trembles and Susannah Edwards were found guilty and hanged. They were the last people to be executed for witchcraft in England. Reading the case it seems

91

that it was a terrible miscarriage of justice. It is so sad, but — '

'But what, Cora?'

Cora made a pained expression. 'There was no transit or anything like that. There was one ten years before. Do you think we could mention that?'

Calum grinned. 'Of course we can use that. We don't make any claims, of course, just mention that it all happened before the Salem Grand Cross. There is no significance in the astrological stuff, as you and I well know, but if the two witch trials are mentioned, we leave it up to our readers' minds to make the connection. Take it from me; the one they will remember will be the local one. That is brilliant, Cora. Brilliant!'

Cora gave another little shrug of her shoulders and smiled demurely as she turned her notebook to another snippet that she had jotted down. 'That's it,' she said, picking up her iPhone and quickly finding the appropriate page on the Internet. She read it and nodded. 'Well, if we need even more local colour, we could say that the last witch executed in Scotland was in 1727 at Dornoch in the Highlands. She was said to have turned her daughter into a horse.'

'I don't suppose there was any astrological event at that time?'

'I couldn't find one, but there is something that you might find interesting.'

'Out with it, lassie. You've got me on bated breath.'

'Her name was Horne. She was known as Jenny Horne, but her real name was Janet. Apparently Jenny was a kind of generic name for a witch back then.'

Calum jumped from his seat and gave her a big kiss on the cheek. 'Tell me, did you get all that information from that wee clicky-box phone?'

'From my iPhone, yes! It's brilliant,' she enthused. 'It does everything; lets me onto the Internet, pick up emails wherever I am, satellite maps and, of course, it is a digital camera and video recorder all rolled into one.'

'Hmm, maybe I should get one. Brilliant it may be, but I think you are a genius, Cora. I love you!' Then he stared at her, realizing that he had declared his feelings.

She kissed him back. 'And I love you too, my darling. But wait, I have another idea. You know the Sentinel Stone?'

'Up on the moor overlooking the harbour? Of course I know it. Torquil, Ralph and I used to climb on it when we were kids. What about it?'

'I asked my great-aunt Bella. There was an

old legend that witches used to meet there, like the hags in Macbeth.'

'Faith! How did I forget that?' Calum said, smacking his forehead with the flat of his hand. 'The Hag Stone, it used to be called. I think the name went when everyone went PC.'

'It's a link, though, don't you think?'

He kissed her hard.

She giggled, and the kissing continued.

II

Tam MacOnachie was in a state of agitation when Torquil arrived at the harbour. A mist had come in and it felt as if it could rain soon.

'I've taped off the area, Inspector McKinnon,' he said, as Torquil dismounted from his Bullet and pulled off his helmet and gauntlets. 'I was a bit worried that it would rain.'

'Have you actually touched it, Tam?'

Tam MacOnachie's eyebrows rose scornfully. 'Are you seriously asking me that, Torquil McKinnon? I am an experienced harbour master and I am quite aware of the significance of finding an object with blood on it on my harbour.'

He led the way to the area that was already taped off, but which he had extended to include the piles of lobster creels that were adjacent to the area where they had examined Dr Horne's body.

'If you stand on the capstan you'll see over the top. It's lying there. My guess is that whoever hit the poor woman just tossed it over there.'

Torquil hopped on top of the capstan and peered over the creels. A bloodstained empty glass wine or cordial bottle, he couldn't determine which because the label was covered in blood, was lying on top of a creel.

'Possibly, Tam. It is looking more and more likely. I'll get Morag and Ewan down here to photograph everything and get it out. They'll need to dismantle all those creels one by one. It'll be a bit like doing a jigsaw. Each one will have to be examined for any clues, or blood. Then we'll need to get the blood checked to see if it is Dr Horne's.'

He hopped down and phoned Morag.

'Aye, you'll need to go over the whole lot, one by one,' he told her. 'Tam MacOnachie has very rightly extended the taped area. We'd better be quick, though. If it rains then the blood — assuming it is blood — could be washed away.'

'Tell her that some of the folk are not too pleased,' the harbour master said loudly, leaning towards Torquil. 'It is impinging on the harbour and it isn't making it easy for folk to get to their boats.'

Torquil pointedly moved away along the harbour, leaving Tam standing with his hands in the pockets of his brown shop-coat, tapping one of his Wellington boots in a puddle.

When Torquil had finished he came back to join him. 'There is something else I meant to ask you about, Tam.'

'Ask anything you want, Inspector.'

'Are you aware that the buoys at the Cruadalach Isles had been cut?'

Tam MacOnachie's jaw dropped. 'Cut? Are you sure?'

'So the Drummond twins said. They'll need to be replaced quickly. We don't want another accident like the kayak.'

'Ach, it is high time that Trinity House had proper sea-bed tied, heavy-duty Isolated Danger Mark buoys put down there. They seem to think that just because there isn't much at the Cruadalach Isles and that commercial boats avoid them, that there is no real danger. But this accident that the lassie had was just waiting to happen, in my opinion.' He eyed Torquil icily. 'Why did nobody tell me?'

'Point taken, Tam. You should have been told.'

The harbour master sighed. 'Well, I'd better get out there and have a look.'

96

'You do that, but don't touch them. They are on a wee dune there, but now that we have this situation here, I think we might need to take a closer look at them as well. I'll arrange that with the Drummond boys. All I want you to do is put out new ones. Can you do that?'

Eggy MacOnachie gave him a stern look. 'The expression about not teaching your granny to suck eggs comes to mind, Inspector.'

III

Douglas met Rosie outside the Masonic Arms Hotel. They embraced and kissed. Relative to their parting kiss on the threshold of the hotel the night before it was a chaste exchange.

'You have heard the bad news, then?' Douglas asked.

Rosie grimaced and nodded. 'We heard over breakfast. I can hardly believe it. What happened, I wonder? Do you think she slipped, or what?'

Douglas bit his lip. 'I'm not supposed to say anything, but it looks suspicious.'

Rosie gasped. 'You don't mean . . . ?'

He nodded. 'She might have been clouted on the head and then dumped in the water. I guess the news will be full of it soon.'

'Couldn't she have just fallen and bumped her head, then fallen in? An accident?'

'She'd have had to fall over the sea wall. It's too high to stumble over and it's pretty thick.'

'Oh my God, that is terrible. And she was so alive at the lecture last night. She was in the Bonnie Prince Charlie last night as well, but I don't think she was over-imbibing.'

'I must admit I didn't notice, Rosie. My attention was elsewhere.'

She elbowed him in the ribs then smiled. 'You had my attention too, you lovely big man.' She squeezed his hand. 'So what about this trip you said you were going to take me on this morning?'

Douglas clicked his teeth. 'Actually, I'm afraid we're going to have to take a rain check on that. Until we have a clearer picture about what happened last night my inspector has said he needs all hands on deck. And in my brother's and my case that could just about mean anything. We're specials, so we are at the bottom of the pecking order. We get the jobs that no one else wants.'

'That's a pity. I was looking forward to spending the morning alone with you.' She sighed and, reaching up, kissed his cheek. 'But maybe this evening?'

'Try and keep me away. So have you any idea of what you'll do with the day?'

'I'll go and see the chandler, I think. See exactly how long he'll be mending my kayak.'

Douglas looked worried. 'And what does that mean? Will you be straight off with the others? With Henry and whatsisname?'

Rosie could not fail to notice the edge in his voice. 'I'm not sure, Douglas. We are all on holiday together and we had plans.'

'And they don't include a West Uist fisherman-cum-special police constable?'

'Well, they didn't yesterday.'

'Will he put pressure on you?'

'I take it you mean Jerome? Well, frankly, they both might, but I'm a big girl and I make my own decisions. At one time Jerome and I were together, but now it is another matter.'

'But he still likes you. He's pretty possessive, you know.'

'Are you getting jealous?' she asked coyly.

'Frankly, aye!'

She squeezed his hand again. 'My big knight errant. You have no need to be jealous. I think I like West Uist more and more. And I like you, Douglas.'

The sliding doors opened and Henry Dodds and Jerome Morton came out.

'Ah, Rosie, so that is why you dashed off so quickly,' Henry Dodds said with a grin. 'Good morning, Douglas.'

'Don't you think we should do a bit of

work now that we have the chance?' Jerome asked her, ignoring Douglas.

'I have plans, Jerome,' Rosie replied.

'And I had better go,' said Douglas, kissing her on the lips. 'I'll ring when I'm free.' And bidding them all an affable farewell he left.

'Just what are you playing at?' Jerome challenged, once Douglas was well out of earshot.

Rosie scowled at him, 'Don't worry. I know exactly what I am doing.'

Henry pre-empted any reply by Jerome. 'And I am utterly sure that you do, Rosie. As for me, I am off as well.' He grinned. 'And it might involve seeing a lady.'

IV

Murdoch drove the Star Wagon along Harbour Street and parked outside Tam MacOnachie's chandlery.

He got out and came round the van to meet Gavin as he got out of the passenger side, hauling out his big camera.

'I cannot say that I feel easy about you filming where Dr Horne died,' Murdoch said, as they walked over to the open door of the chandlery.

'I can't afford to miss the opportunity of a slot on Scottish TV news, Murdoch. You know that. The more I can put on my CV the better.'

'It must be pretty full already, what with your two degrees, your astronomy primer and those two science fiction novels.'

'Ah, you know that I am finished with fiction writing, Murdoch. That's why I am focusing on my filming. I fancy making a proper documentary sometime and the more news slots I can get the better chance I will have to get serious financial backing.'

Murdoch nodded. He was all too well aware that Gavin had felt the need to throw himself into work. As an ambitious man himself, he understood.

Tam MacOnachie was busy in the workshop at the back of the chandlery and he came out when Murdoch pressed the buzzer on the counter.

'Ah, good morning, Mr Jamieson,' he said. 'I always watch your show. I guess that most seafaring types do. The stars are an important part of our lives, for all the modern technology that boats have nowadays.'

Murdoch beamed. 'Of course, the ancient mariner's art.'

'But not so much of the ancient!' returned Tam with a smug laugh, delighted as he was at his own wit.

'A bad business this morning,' Gavin said. 'Can you tell us about it and maybe give us a wee interview for Scottish TV? I hope that I can get a slot on the news today.'

Tam's face lit up. 'An interview? Me, on TV? Well, I don't know about that.'

'It would be a public service,' Gavin said.

'Will you be interviewing me, Mr Jamieson?'

Murdoch hesitated, but Gavin was quick to reply. 'That is a great idea. Go on, Murdoch. Getting you on the news will reinforce the message that you are here filming the transit and the conjunctions.'

'In that case, yes, Mr MacOnachie. I will be interviewing you.'

'Then you should call me Tam.'

'Right, Tam,' Murdoch said. 'So can you show us where it all happened?'

Tam signalled and they followed him down onto the harbour to the taped-off area. He stopped and turned. 'Of course, you realize that I cannot say very much, considering that the police are investigating. They think it is suspicious, you know.'

'So we heard,' Gavin said. 'In what way?'

'Well, I don't think I'm giving much away in saying that Dr Horne's body was found floating in the water and that after she had been pulled out of the water by one of our local policemen it was found that she had a head injury.'

'Any idea how she got it?' Murdoch asked.

Tam's eyes narrowed shrewdly. 'You'd better ask the police about that.'

'We'll do that as well,' Gavin replied. 'The more little snippets we can get the better.'

'Oh, well, then you'd maybe better take a picture of the chalk marks that they found.' And he directed their attention to the wavy lines chalked on the wall beside the creels.

Murdoch and Gavin looked at each other.

'Are you thinking what I'm thinking, Gavin?'

'An astrological sign?'

Tam coughed. 'Inspector McKinnon was very interested in those. And I think he had the same idea as you two.'

'That is interesting, Tam. Very interesting,' said Murdoch. 'Now, I think we have all we need for an interview. Just pretend that the camera isn't there and we'll have a little chat about what we talked about.'

Tam immediately pulled in his stomach and stood as straight as he could. He had heard that television makes most people look a few pounds heavier. He wanted to look his best for his television debut.

V

Melissa Mathieson had managed to get her friends to leave, and was about to put up the closed sign and nip down to the harbour to see if she could find out more about what had happened from Tam MacOnachie when the door opened and Henry Dodds walked in.

'Oh, I am sorry, I was just about to . . . '

Henry beamed at her. 'To leave? Oh, that is a pity; I was hoping to have a word. I wanted to catch up about last night.'

He stood looking around the softly lit shop with its bookcases of astrological and paranormal titles, the shelves of candles, crystals, aromatic oils and racks of alternative remedies. The ceiling was garlanded with silks, pinned up by their four corners and pinned in the middle so that it looked as if they were cushions, with dream-catchers arranged like dangling tassels.

'Is it a reading you wanted? The tarot, i ching or the palm? I also do the oracle or just a straight clairvoyant reading. You could come back later if you wished. The thing is that there has been something of a tragedy this morning. A friend of mine has died and I — '

'Yes, very sad. I heard about Dr Horne's death at breakfast.'

Melissa nodded. It irritated her slightly that he was being so persistent in his attentions, especially in light of the tragedy. She decided to pretend that he had failed to really register with her. 'You were at her lecture last night, weren't you?'

'Yes and I came and talked to you and Dr Horne for a few moments in the Bonnie Prince Charlie.' He smiled ruefully. 'But that is the story of my life. People don't notice me, or they take me for granted. It is a hazard of being a literary agent.'

Melissa feigned sudden recognition. 'Of course, you are Rosie Barton and Jerome Morton's agent.'

She snapped her fingers and pointed to one of the bookcases in the far end of the shop. 'I have several of their titles. They sell quite well, although I have to say that they do not always come to the correct conclusions, in my opinion.'

'It was your opinion I wanted to consult you about,' Henry went on. 'You see, I understand that you are a writer yourself.'

Melissa flushed slightly. 'In a small way. I edit a psychic magazine and I write a clairvoyant and angel therapy blog.'

'I know, I have seen them. I wondered if you had thought of writing a book yourself?'

She shook her head. 'No, never. I am not sure that I have enough knowledge to write a whole book.'

Henry pulled out his wallet and handed her a business card. 'That is where a good agent can often help. An agent has many roles, one of them being to act like a catalyst to stimulate ideas. I am sure that if you are interested, I could broker a book deal for you. Perhaps you'd like to think about it and then give me a ring. Perhaps I could buy you supper or a drink?'

Melissa glanced at the card and tucked it into the breast pocket of her purple blouse. She smiled. 'Those are three very tempting offers and I will consider them all very carefully. But now I really must go.'

'Of course,' said Henry with his hand on the doorhandle. He smiled. 'Just ring. I am always on call for my authors.'

He opened the door and turned back. 'And if that won't work, perhaps I had better get you to see what is in my stars.'

He was still smiling as he left and walked along the street.

By contrast, Melissa Mathieson's smile had disappeared the moment the door closed.

VI

Torquil was in his office trying to bring himself up to speed on Dr Janet Home's biography. He had despatched Morag and Ewan to retrieve the bottle and do the necessary forensics on the area around the creels. And he had

106

sent the Drummond twins out to the Cruadalach Isles to take photographs of the buoys that had been cut and to look for any clues as to who could have done it. Not that he expected there to be any.

The phone went and he answered it, almost intuitively knowing that it would be Superintendent Lumsden.

'Right, McKinnon, what sort of unholy disaster have you brought down on us this time?'

'Excuse me, Superintendent?'

'Spill the beans, McKinnon. What is going on? Sergeant Golspie has told me that you have fished the body of some celebrity astronomer out of the harbour.'

'Not an astronomer, Superintendent. An astrologer. Dr Janet Horne was found in Kyleshiffin harbour this morning and PC Ewan McPhee pulled her out.'

There was a snort down the phone. 'So that hammer-throwing oaf is of some use, then.'

Torquil felt his temper begin to stir. 'Ewan McPhee is not an oaf, Superintendent. He is — '

'Yes, yes, yes! It was just an expression. Get on with it. So this astrologer was found dead. You have reported it to the procurator fiscal. A post-mortem has been arranged, I hope.'

'We are awaiting the results.'

'Why, is it suspicious?'

'She had a head injury.'

'So it could have been an accident, or someone could have thumped her? OK. Any sexual suspicion? Was she raped?'

'No sign of that on the external examination, sir.'

There was silence for a moment, broken only by a tapping noise as if Superintendent Lumsden was drumming his fingers on the desk.

'Look here, McKinnon, you and I have not seen eye to eye on a lot of things in the past. I have doubts about you at times. I think that station of yours is lax and your staff are undisciplined.'

'With respect, Superintendent, that is nonsense.'

'And with respect, Inspector McKinnon, you seem to attract an inordinate amount of attention to West Uist. It is not good for my crime figures.'

'Again, with respect, sir, our crime figures are very good. We solve our crimes.'

'Yes, but there are still too bloody many crimes and suspicious goings-on. I want you to crack down on it, McKinnon.'

Torquil clenched his teeth but said nothing.

'Prevention, that must be the key word,

McKinnon. You need to be more proactive and start preventing things like this from happening.'

'I don't quite understand, sir. Are you suggesting that this event, whether it was an accident or worse, could have been prevented?'

'Exactly!'

'Well, sir, if that is the case perhaps I could do with more staff. I only have a desk sergeant, one constable and two special constables.'

'Those fishermen twins! They are hardly special.'

Torquil almost smiled. 'Perhaps we should have a crime prevention officer like other places, Superintendent. Could I suggest that Sergeant Golspie be sent back to work with us, sir?'

'Don't be insubordinate, McKinnon. And don't try to outmanoeuvre me. I could have you for breakfast any day of the week. You bloody well cannot have Sergeant Golspie, because she is needed here. Now, here is what I want you to do. I want you to keep me fully in the picture. I don't want to hear what is happening whenever I turn on the television. I want to know about any developments before the media. Is that clear?'

'As clear as crystal, Superintendent.'

As usual the phone went dead without any pleasantries.

After leaving the church Lachlan had taken Crusoe back to the manse with the intention of writing his next sermon. But after feeding the dog and watching him curl up in his basket at the end of the hall, he had been tempted to do a little work on the Excelsior Talisman Twin Sports motorcycle that he and Torquil had been slowly rebuilding. Alongside the wall, a line of oil-stained newspapers protected the parquet floor from the assortment of carburettor components, oil filters and gears.

He took off his jacket and rolled up his sleeves, then settled down on the floor and opened his toolkit. Soon his mind had moved from spiritual thoughts to images of how the classic motorcycle would perform once they finally reassembled it.

Playing the bagpipes and classic motorcycles were two of the passions that he and Torquil shared. The Excelsior Talisman project had been going on in an enthusiastic but non-productive manner for at least a couple of years.

Although they both wanted to see the bike up and road-worthy, while it remained a collection of spare parts they both unconsciously felt that the manse was their home.

And yet Lachlan appreciated only too well that soon there would be talk of wedding plans, and then they would want to find a home of their own.

Och, Lachlan, he chided himself. It will be a good thing for the pair of them. You'll just have to get used to living on your own.

Crusoe whimpered and Lachlan looked over to see him sleeping. His paws were twitching and his ears flapped back and forth.

'I am guessing that you are chasing rabbits in dreamland,' he whispered. 'But I will miss you too, my wee friend, when you go.'

And, as he said it, he thought of Dr Horne's sudden death and the unpredictability of life.

'Last night at the lecture the poor woman wouldn't have thought that she would be dead this morning.' He shook his head. 'I am sure that Murdoch is feeling a bit upset about the words he had with her as well.'

And it was strange, he thought, the way that Rosie Barton had in turn challenged Murdoch, causing his hasty exit.

'What was that all about, Murdoch?' he said, to the first of the two carburettors that he had begun to strip down. 'She seemed angry at you, right enough. What was it she said — something about academic credibility?'

He whistled as he made a mental note to ask his old friend about it later.

VIII

Torquil had just made himself a cup of tea and had returned to his computer search when Ralph McLelland phoned.

'I still have to analyse some of the samples, but I thought you ought to have a preliminary report. There was a basal fracture of her skull, consistent with that bruising and the bloody wound at the back of the head. She had a whopper of a bleed into the back of the skull and a contrecoup injury to the front of the brain.'

'What does that mean, Ralph?'

'It means that she had an injury to the front of the brain as well.'

'Was she hit twice, then?'

'No. It was a single blow, but the brain is a bit like a lump of jelly. If you hit the skull hard the brain will bounce to the opposite side of the skull and rupture blood vessels there. We call it a contrecoup contusion.'

'Is that very significant.'

'It means that the trauma was huge. It was almost certainly a killing blow.'

'Could it have been accidental?'

'Hard to imagine that. If she had fallen and bashed her head I cannot see how she would have pitched forward and ended up in the harbour.'

'Did that kill her, then? Or did she drown?'

'That is another tricky question. She has some plankton in her lungs, but her heart would have been pumping for a while, I think. I suspect that she received a blow to the back of the head and that was sufficient to propel her forward into the water, or she was knocked out and then thrown in.'

'But either way, it is bad.'

'It is bad, Torquil. In my opinion there is no doubt, she was killed by someone.'

'Aye, well, Morag and Ewan should be with you soon with that bottle I told you about. They will have photographed it *in situ*. The biggest question we need answering — '

'I know. Whether it is her blood or not? I'll have a blood sample ready for them so they can send it to the forensic lab in Dundee with the bottle.'

'It won't have been dusted for fingerprints so you'll be careful, won't you, Ralph?'

'Of course. In the vast majority of cases where a bottle is used as a bludgeon the bottle neck is used as a handle, so that's where they'll find prints, I expect.'

'But will you see if it could be a possible murder weapon?'

'From what you've already told me, if I was a betting man, I'd say it was odds-on favourite.'

6

I

Ming McDonald had been an inshore fisherman for most of his life. He was proud of his work although he bemoaned the fact that the fleet that had once numbered thirty boats had now shrunk to a mere eight vessels. Like all the other fishermen he went out whenever the weather and the sea allowed it, and fished for whatever was available.

In his eight-metre creel boat the *Sea Eagle* he fished for prawns, langoustines, lobsters and crabs. He would drop ten strings of pots; twelve pots to a string, and leave them marked off with his buoys for a couple of days at a time, harvesting them in time for Melrose the fish merchant's thrice-weekly buying trip. On the other days he would go out with his nets and try for herring, red mullet and occasionally monkfish. These he divided between Melrose and the local fishmongers, including his cousin's stall, which was open every Tuesday and Saturday on Harbour Street market.

It was because of Tam MacOnachie's antipathy towards his boat and his tendency to stack his creels the way that he did, that a feud had grown up between McDonald and the harbour master. Or at least, it had done in Ming's eyes. Other fishermen like the Drummond twins seemed to get away with anything, despite the fact that they were as rude as sin to MacOnachie.

Along with his fishing business, McDonald also ran sightseeing and dolphin-watching trips during the holiday season. When Tam insisted that he refrained from putting his advertising board beside the *Sea Eagle's* berth and only have it on the harbour wall on Harbour Street, McDonald had blown a fuse. They had rowed very publicly. Then the harbour master had lately taken it upon himself to distribute penalty tickets for tying up at other berths or for piling his creels too far along the harbour. That had been like showing a red rag to a bull. He was determined that he would somehow or other get rid of the harbour master. So far he had been unsuccessful in getting people to listen to him.

The man's a useless fool, he mused to himself as he chewed the end of his unlit cigar and steered out to sea. He looked out of the bridge and grinned as he ran through the Warner 2:1 gearbox and the Perkins Sabre 130 engine powered the little vessel through the waves.

And now he's bragging about how he's going to be on the news about that woman's death.

Pulling out a lighter he lit his cigar and relished the taste of the smoke. He looked at the glowing end of the cigar and grinned. 'He'd better be careful, or one day he'll get burned.'

And he began to laugh.

II

Morag and Ewan spent almost an hour at the scene, meticulously photographing, gridding and then removing the creels one by one. They labelled them all, took a picture of each one and then restacked them to the side. When they eventually gained access to the bottle they dealt with it in as delicate a manner as possible, being careful to photograph it from every angle before bagging it so that it could be sent off to the forensics in Dundee.

'Torquil wants it to get there as soon as possible,' Morag said, once they had finished and were preparing to leave.

'The ferry will take hours,' Ewan replied. 'I could take the *Seaspray* if you want, but again it will take me time.'

'Torquil said he has arranged with Lorna for the helicopter to come from Benbecula. That way it keeps the superintendent in the loop.'

'So that means we need to meet it at the cottage hospital. You'll want me to go, I suppose.'

Morag tweaked his cheek. She always felt like a big sister to Ewan, as well as being his sergeant. 'No, my dear, I'll do that. It will give me an opportunity to let Ralph McLelland see whether it could have been used to knock Dr Horne on the head. At the same time I need to collect a sample of her blood to go to forensics along with it.'

Ewan heaved a sigh of relief. 'You are a star, Morag Driscoll, that is what you are. The smell of that mortuary is enough to put me off food for days.'

'Well, we can't have that, now, can we? So, you get back to the station and see if the boss needs anything more doing and I'll be back when I can.'

They walked back along the quay and were met by Tam.

'You are finished, then, are you?'

'All done, Mr MacOnachie,' replied Morag. 'I hear you are going to be on the news tonight.'

'Aye, just doing my civic duty, ye know.'

'It is a bad business,' Ewan said.

'Aye, and very disruptive, too. I don't like the harbour being tied up like this for too long. Folk find it difficult to get to their boats with all these taped-off areas.' He pointed to

118

the neatly stacked creels which had been moved further down the harbour. 'I must say that you've made a better job of them than their owner.'

Morag eyed him quizzically for a moment. 'Oh, you mean the creels? Whose are they?'

Tam MacOnachie blew air through his lips. 'Och, just the bane of my life! They are Ming McDonald's.'

III

Wallace and Douglas had chugged out towards the Cruadalach Isles in what for them was relative silence. Normally they had a good banter all the time, but today they were both reluctant to talk because the topic of conversation would inevitably come round to Rosie Barton.

But, at last, Wallace could hold out no more.

'Out with it then, little brother, is this the big one?'

Douglas sniffed disdainfully. 'Enough of the *little brother*! You are a mere fifteen minutes older than me, as well you know.'

'Aye, well, they say that in those first few minutes of life the brain develops at an incredible rate. Let's just say that my brain is more mature. And that being the case, little

Brother, I have more experience than you. And so I repeat, is this the big one?'

Despite himself Douglas grinned. 'You know, I think maybe it is. It is early days, of course, but Rosie and I just seem to click.'

'We've been here before, remember? Are you sure that it isn't just lust? She's a stunner, I have to admit.'

Douglas eyed him askance. 'You are not trying to tell me something, are you, Bruv?'

'Like what?'

'Like you fancy her yourself!'

'Easy, Douglas. We both know the unwritten rule and so far we have both abided by it. But rest easy, anyway. Stunning she may be, but she is more your type than mine.'

Douglas nodded. In so many ways they thought and acted in almost exactly the same way, but in matters of attraction they inexplicably had quite different preferences. He had always been attracted to blondes, while Wallace had a liking for redheads.

'I know, I've fallen in love pretty easily once or twice,' Douglas began.

'Or say fifteen times and counting,' Wallace interjected with a grin.

'A few times, anyway,' Douglas conceded. 'But so have you.'

'Precisely my point, Brother. Just don't get too embroiled, especially not at a time like this. Not when we have a potential murder investigation on our hands.'

'Are you saying that I'm not focused?'

Wallace pointed through the cabin window. 'Well, we are getting awfully close to the Cruadalach Isles and they have no buoys, remember.'

Douglas scowled and slowed the engine and they coasted in. They anchored and then they both jumped down into the shallows.

'The footprints are all still here from the other day,' Wallace said, bending down to examine them. He pulled out his digital camera and began taking pictures.

'And there are only mine leading over to the sand dune and the buoys,' said Douglas.

He waited for Wallace to photograph the tracks and the dune, then they both went over to the buoys and Wallace photographed them, zooming in to take close-ups of the cut ropes on the four heavy-duty, bright orange polyurethane buoys.

'Whoever cut them hurled them over here,' Douglas pointed out. 'That is no mean task since they weigh a fair bit.'

'But why would anyone do something so stupid?'

'Search me,' Douglas replied. 'But maybe we should take these back for Torquil to have a look at?'

'No, he said to leave them here. He said that Eggy would be coming out to put up new ones, whenever he could get away.'

Douglas pointed towards West Uist. 'Unless I am mistaken that is him on his way now.'

'I suppose we should wait and give him a hand.'

'Aye, it might be good for a laugh.'

Wallace grinned. 'Maybe it isn't the big love affair that I thought, after all. Last time you fell in love I could barely get you out in the boat for an honest day's fishing.'

Douglas playfully punched him on the arm. 'You know what they say: man cannot live by love alone. And what could be better than whetting one's appetite with a bit of Eggy-baiting?'

IV

Ewan had returned to the station and taken over the desk from Torquil just moments before Murdoch Jamieson and Gavin McIntyre came in to request an interview and a statement about Dr Horne's death.

'Ah, that had better be my boss, Inspector McKinnon, that you speak to. I'll see if he is available.'

Torquil had groaned when Ewan told him,

but had immediately come through from his office.

'Ah, Torquil, what can you tell us?' Murdoch asked. 'It is dreadful news.'

'And — er — could you say something on camera for us?' Gavin asked. 'I want to get this all done and in the can for the Scottish TV evening news. We already interviewed Mr MacOnachie.'

Torquil considered for a moment then nodded his head. 'OK, but all that I can say at this moment is that we are treating the death as suspicious.'

'Which means that it is a murder investigation?' Murdoch asked.

'I repeat, it means that we are treating it as suspicious. I won't say more than that at the moment. We need an official result from the post-mortem examination and other tests.'

'We saw some strange chalk marks on the harbour,' Murdoch told him. 'Mr MacOnachie, the harbour master, showed them to us. They looked like astrological markings for Aquarius.'

'We noticed that and we have taken those into account. They may or may not be of relevance.'

'And we believe that you have found a possible weapon.'

Torquil raised a quizzical eyebrow. 'Where did you hear that?'

Murdoch smiled. 'Torquil, please don't misunderstand me. I am not an investigative journalist; I am, in fact, not a journalist at all: I am an astronomy presenter who just happens to be on the island with his cameraman. This is simply an opportunistic news piece that Gavin has persuaded me to do. The truth is that Mr MacOnachie implied that you might have found something, but he was quite evasive.'

Torquil smiled. He knew how much of a martinet Eggy MacOnachie could be. 'Let me just say that we have been conducting investigations around the harbour.'

Murdoch smiled. 'So be it. Just a short official statement then. I'll ask a couple of questions and set it up for you.'

Ewan watched through the kitchen door, which he had left ajar. He sipped his tea and nodded admiringly at the way Torquil conducted himself under the glare of the camera. He was glad that he did not have to be exposed to public scrutiny like that. Stepping up on the podium to receive his wrestling and hammer-throwing prizes at the Western Isles Games was one thing: shouldering the responsibility for an investigation on national television was quite another. Not only was Ewan McPhee slightly squeamish, he was also camera-shy.

V

Melissa Mathieson had not known Janet Horne for long, yet she had respected her work and felt that she had gained understanding about the way that the universe worked by reading her books and discussing with her the significance of the various types of planetary transits.

'How on earth did we not see this coming?' she asked her friends, as they sat sipping herbal tea at a corner table of the Lavender Box, their favourite café at the junction of Bonnygate with Harbour Street.

After visiting the scene of Janet's untimely and tragic death she had called Nettie, who had in turn arranged for their other friends to convene at the café. There were four of them, all kindred spirits, who had formed a friendship over the last few years. Although they came from different spiritual persuasions and were of different ages and seemed very different in most ways, they all shared a deep understanding about spirituality.

Following Melissa's lead they had formed the West Uist Astrological Society, of which they were the committee. The membership had grown surprisingly quickly and they had organized various events throughout the year, including the proposed series of lectures by

Dr Horne to coincide with the transit and the Grand Cross.

Nettie Grant was a middle-aged woman dressed in black from head to toe. She was a native of Bara who had married a ferryman and moved to West Uist, only to become a widow after a couple of years. She had started to wear black clothes then and never shed what people assumed to be her widow's weeds. In truth they reflected the fact that she had discovered Wicca, which she practised and celebrated as a lone white witch.

Iona Hamblin was a younger woman in her early thirties. She was something of a modern hippy who usually wore flowery dresses and tied up her hair with brightly coloured bandannas. She bit her lip and shook her head.

'But we did see it coming,' Agnes Frazer said, sitting forward with her eyes wide open. She was the last of their little clique. A Goth in her mid-twenties with a penchant for body piercings, she had a passion for all things to do with vampires and carried a sample of her boyfriend's blood in a small vial which hung from a chain and disappeared into her cleavage. 'Last night Dr Horne explained all about it herself. The Grand Cross has started to produce its effect: the horrors have started.'

Melissa normally controlled the meetings, but she was feeling very shaken. 'What do you mean, the horrors?'

'The Salem witch trials occurred the last time we had this combination of events.'

'If she was killed by someone, then it must have been the action of a nutter,' Melissa said. 'She was a lovely woman. Who would want to harm her? I mean, it is not as if we lived in such unenlightened days today.'

'I don't know,' Nettie replied. 'People are still pretty unenlightened. Especially on an island like this, tucked away from civilization. And I can't say that I like the idea of a witch trial, on account of me being one.'

She gave a short laugh and then sat back and folded her arms defensively.

All four of them sat and looked from one to the other, each conscious of the same anxiety.

After a few moments Iona broke the silence. 'I know what we should do: we should hold a vigil for Janet. Each of us pray for her in our own way.'

'That's a great idea,' Melissa said.

'We could do it through the night,' Agnes agreed.

'But where should we hold it?' Nettie asked. 'Here in Kyleshiffin? At the harbour, perhaps?'

Melissa shook her head. 'I agree that we

127

should do it somewhere outside, but it should be somewhere more spiritual. What about the Sentinel Stone up on Kyleshiffin Moor?'

Nettie clapped her hands. 'Of course! And it is so very appropriate, since you can see the harbour from there.'

'It is perfect,' agreed Melissa.

A bell tinkled as the door of the café opened and Murdoch Jamieson and Gavin McIntyre came in. They were greeted by Rhona Burns, the proprietor, but rather than taking the table she indicated, after a quick word of explanation to her, they came straight over to the foursome's table.

'We are so sorry to hear about Dr Horne's tragic death,' Murdoch said. 'The thing is, we are taking the opportunity of putting a special series of mini-interviews together for Scottish TV News. It should help the police get to the bottom of this awful thing. Would you be so kind as to record a few words about her?'

Almost as one the four women agreed.

'Just as long as there are no cheap jibes about astrology,' Melissa added.

VI

Ming McDonald had worked hard. He had laid his strings of creels and then gone off to do some net fishing. He had secured a good catch of herrings and taken a couple of monkfish. Then he had gone in search of jellyfish.

Catching and studying jellyfish was something of a passion with him. It had started as a hobby, but of late it had almost become an obsession. Although his academic qualifications were undistinguished, he regarded himself as being of above average intelligence.

'I have certainly got more savvy than that galoot, Tam MacOnachie,' he said to himself, as he gingerly manoeuvred his jellyfish catch into the special container he kept in the hold of the *Sea Eagle*.

'He doesn't know one end of a boat from the other. The man's a bodger, no other word for it. The sooner he goes, the better it will be for all the users of Kyleshiffin harbour.'

He surveyed his catch and assessed that there had to be something of the order of thirty or forty blue jellyfish and maybe a half-dozen of his favourites, the large yellow-brown ones called Lion's Mane, because of their resemblance to the mane of the king of the beasts. Each one was at least a yard in diameter. Among his catch he also found, to his delight, a Portuguese Man-o'-War and a couple of specimens of the purple translucent one that they called Night Light, on account of its ability to glow in the dark. Both of the latter were jellyfish normally found in tropical and subtropical waters, but he had noted that over the last few years they were regularly found in the Atlantic waters around West Uist.

'A good few stingers there, aren't you all? The sea will be a bit safer without you. They say it is global warming that is bringing you all up here, but I have my own theories and I mean to prove it.'

He took his cigar from his mouth and proudly pronounced their biological names. '*Cyanea capillata* and *Pelagia noctiluca*. You are beautiful creatures with beautiful names that fairly trip off the tongue. I'll just take you home first, then I'll go back to the harbour and unload my proper catch.'

Having emptied his net and covered the hold he set off round the island to his house at Gull Cove where he lived alone. The water was deep and he could take his boat right up and tie her up at his very own jetty. He liked living there, out of sight of prying eyes so that he could get on and do his own thing.

It took him two trips back and forth with his wheelbarrow to unload his catch of jellyfish into the large tanks that he kept in his outhouse.

He watched as the Lion's Mane jellyfish swirled after he dumped them in, then separated and settled to the bottom, lying one on top of the other like great thick jelly pancakes.

He pulled out a ledger and jotted a few figures down. He then consulted an ephemeris, a book of the planetary movements. As he did so a thought occurred to him.

Heavens above! That's it! I should have a word with that one-eyed astronomer chappie and his sidekick. They were in the Bonnie Prince Charlie the other night. Maybe they will be interested in my theory.

He winked at the tanks full of jellyfish then set off down the jetty to his boat. First things first. I'd better get the fish off to market.

VII

Jerome Morton and Henry Dodds had been busy all afternoon working on the outline of the new book. It was something that the three of them often did, since both Jerome and Rosie respected Henry's opinions and his ability to think outside the box. On several occasions he had not only been useful in suggesting an area of research, but had also sometimes given them the idea for a book. It was an entirely symbiotic arrangement, since they all benefited from it.

Rosie's whirlwind romance with Special

131

Constable Douglas Drummond had greatly amused Henry, but been a source of intense irritation for Jerome.

When Rosie had failed to show up by four o'clock Jerome decided to try and force the issue by getting her kayak repaired. And since that meant putting some pressure on Tam MacOnachie, he insisted that Henry Dodds should accompany him to the chandlery on the harbour.

But, as it happened, Tam MacOnachie was clearly not a man to be browbeaten.

'I will do what I can, when I can, Mr — er — Horton.'

'That's Morton, not Horton,' Jerome retorted irritably as he talked to Tam across the counter of the chandlery. 'Rosie Barton and I write books, you know. Bestsellers!'

'Is that so, Mr Morton?'

'We are busy people. Influential people.'

'Really? Influential with whom, Mr Morton? Are you saying that I should be influenced to get the kayak done ahead of everything else that needs doing around here? We had a terrible incident, as you know. Dr Horne lost her life in my harbour and I consider that assisting the police and the authorities comes ahead of fixing a kayak.'

Henry had been standing behind Jerome, quietly enjoying Jerome's discomfiture and

132

the way that he was trying unsuccessfully to bully the harbour master. His attention drifted out of the door. He saw the group of women led by Melissa Mathieson come out of the Lavender Box café.

He waited until they had almost reached the chandlery then dashed out in front of them.

'Ah, good afternoon, ladies,' he said to the group, with one of his most ingratiating smiles. Then almost immediately he focused on Melissa.

'Actually, Dr Mathieson, I am so glad that I caught you. I have something I need to ask you. A professional matter.'

Nettie Grant had responded to Henry's charm and instantly spoke up for the group. 'Then, Melissa, we must not detain you. We have the vigil all planned.'

Melissa looked perturbed. 'Yes, but — '

'But nothing,' replied Nettie. 'It will flow like a charm.' And with a smile she led the others away.

Melissa felt a little piqued as she stared at their backs as they made their way down the road. Why had Nettie left her alone with this man? she wondered.

'Would you care to pop into the chandlery with me?' Henry asked. 'I want you to meet my colleague, Jerome Morton. He's writing a book, you see, and I would love your professional opinion about the book's basic theme.' He placed a hand on her arm. 'And as to that other matter I mentioned earlier, I really would love to have a consultation with you.'

Melissa gently drew her arm away with a smile and walked ahead of him into the chandlery.

She had not been in the shop very often and she ran appraising eyes over the way that Tam had arranged his business. Her impression was one of chaos. Fishing rods large and small, spearguns, boat parts, books, life jackets and all sorts of provisions needed on expeditions near and far. Racks of knives, coils of ropes, anchors and nets vied for every available space of wall and counter.

'Doctor Mathieson, good day,' said Tam.

Melissa graced him with a smile, then before she could give a reply Henry had spun Jerome around and was introducing them.

'Jerome, here is Dr Mathieson, the lady that I told you about.'

Jerome Morton held out a hand and smiled. 'Henry has told me all about you.'

Melissa looked confused. 'I am sorry, but perhaps there has been some mistake. You see, with respect, Mr Dodds knows nothing about me at all.'

Henry Dodds was not remotely nonplussed by her comment. He smiled. 'Which is something I am hoping to put right pretty soon.'

VIII

Cora and Calum had prepared a special edition of the *Chronicle* for the next day and gone to the Bonnie Prince Charlie tavern for a drink and to listen to the Scottish TV news at six o'clock. The bar was heaving as usual and Mollie McFadden and her staff were busily pumping pints of Heather Ale.

Cora managed to get a table in front of the large plasma-screen television while Calum ordered drinks from the bar.

'Half of Kyleshiffin seems to be here,' Calum remarked, after he had weaved his way through the crowd, gathering the usual ribbing and joking from the locals. The background chatter suddenly stopped when the Scottish TV news signature tune came on.

'I heard you had a thing about her,' Cora teased, as the voluptuous Scottish TV anchorwoman Kirstie Macroon appeared.

Calum eyed her uneasily and fumbled with his bow-tie. 'Ah, well, not exactly a thing, Cora. More a kind of . . . of — '

'Infatuation?' she suggested.

He grinned. 'Och, what does that matter? She's not a patch on you, lassie.'

'Really?'

'Aye, really,' he replied, his eyes going glassy as he leaned closer to her.

A hand descended on his shoulder and he twisted round to find Tam MacOnachie peering down at him. 'This is a public place, you know, Calum Steele. Could you and your young lady control your passion and let the rest of us listen to the news?'

Cora blushed and Calum scowled, because he was not entirely sure whether the harbour master was serious or not. A chorus of ribald laughter round about him led him to believe that whether or not it was meant as a joke, the bar crowd had taken it as such, which just made Calum squirm all the more.

Mollie MacFadden rang her bell. 'Right, folk, let's have a bit of hush. I'm sure you all want to hear what's been going on.' And with her other hand she worked the remote control to increase the volume.

Kirstie Macroon's voice, with her soft Galloway accent, filled the room.

'And the whole island of West Uist is now in shock after the body of Dr Janet Horne, the famous astrologer, was found floating in the harbour at Kyleshiffin this morning. We are fortunate in having a film crew on the island, since the equally famous astronomer Murdoch Jamieson is filming his programme *Heavens Above* there at the moment.' She put a hand to her earpiece. 'And I have Murdoch on the line right now. Good evening, Murdoch.'

The shot switched to Murdoch standing by the sea wall overlooking the harbour. One or two of the locals darted to the window to see whether they could see him.

'Good evening, Kirstie. It is a very sad business, I am afraid. The mood here in Kyleshiffin is extremely sombre.'

'Can you tell us anything about the case, Murdoch?'

'Briefly, the local harbour master, Mr Tam MacOnachie, was opening his chandlery this morning at about a quarter to seven. He saw her floating face down in the harbour. As it happened, one of the local police officers was passing and upon being shown the body by Mr MacOnachie, he dived in and pulled her out of the water.

'Sadly, she was pronounced dead when the local physician, Dr Ralph McLelland, was called.

'Earlier today, I interviewed Mr MacOnachie.'

The scene shifted to show Murdoch and Tam MacOnachie outside his chandlery.

'It must have been a dreadful shock, Mr MacOnachie. Could you describe what you saw?'

Everyone in the bar listened to Tam's account. He then described the finding of a blood-stained bottle among the piles of creels and the curious chalk markings on the harbour wall.

As the interview drew to a close the actual Tam took a swig of his half-pint of Heather Ale shandy and nodded appreciatively at all the words of praise about his interview.

'It was a daunting experience, though. It was my first time on television and it couldn't have been a sadder occasion.'

There were murmurs of agreement and utterings of sympathy.

Then on the plasma screen Murdoch Jamieson was again seen by the harbour wall as Kirstie Macroon's voice went on to question him.

'So tell me, Murdoch, what do the police make of this bloodstained bottle?'

'Well, after speaking to Mr MacOnachie I interviewed Inspector Torquil McKinnon.'

Again the shot changed to show Torquil and Murdoch standing in front of the counter in the police station.

'And can you tell us whether you are dealing with a murder case, Inspector McKinnon?'

Torquil's face was pretty dead-pan. 'There are certainly suspicious items found near to the place where Dr Horne's body was found in the water. I am still awaiting the results of a post-mortem examination. At the moment all I can tell you is that we are treating her death as suspicious.'

Once again the shot returned to Murdoch. 'It is all very sad, Kirstie. After I saw Inspector McKinnon I interviewed a number of Dr Horne's friends. They are planning to hold a vigil in memory of her throughout the night at a place called the Sentinel Stone up on Kyleshiffin Moor.'

The scene changed to the café and the meeting with the four women.

'And why have you chosen the moor?' Murdoch asked.

Nettie Grant answered. 'Because the Sentinel Stone is of very special significance to women like Dr Janet Horne and ourselves. We are all spiritual people, women who may have been considered witches in previous centuries. Tonight we shall be praying for and meditating on the meaning of our friend's life.'

'You will be there throughout the whole night?'

'We will, until sunrise.'

Kirstie Macroon appeared in the studio again. She recapped then went on to another piece of news.

Calum Steele picked up his pint and nodded his head. 'Aye, typical of Torquil.

That's what he told us. He won't give much away until he has hard facts to deal with.'

'But how much more does he need?' Cora asked.

'That's a question, right enough,' Calum replied, draining the rest of his beer in one draught. 'The answer is harder to give.' He winked at her then stood up and tapped his glass on the table to catch the attention of the rest of the bar's customers.

'If you want a clear update on the case and some investigative journalistic insight then read the special edition of the *West Uist Chronicle* tomorrow morning, folks.'

Almost immediately several locals descended on him with offers of drinks in exchange for information, which to Cora's disbelief he steadfastly refused.

'That's not like you to refuse a round of drinks, Calum,' she whispered, as he ushered her through the crowd towards the exit.

'Professionalism, lassie! Professionalism! Keep them guessing. We still have to sell papers, after all.'

'Do you think we ought to go up to the moor later and maybe take a picture or two of those ladies and their vigil?'

'Actually, Cora, darling, I sort-of have other plans for us tonight.'

Cora giggled and squeezed his hand.

IX

Torquil and the Padre were sitting down with a dram of Glen Corlan on either side of the fireplace in the sitting room of the manse watching the end of the Scottish TV news.

'Will it take long to get the forensics evidence?' Lachlan asked.

'A day or two. Ralph is pretty sure that she received her head injury before ending up in the water. The bloodstained bottle looks pretty damning, but until we have the clear match we can't say any more than that it was suspicious. I've reported it to the procurator fiscal and a fatal accident inquiry will be called. I just wish . . . '

His mobile phone went off and he saw Laura's number flashing.

'Hi, darling, I am guessing that you saw the news?' he asked.

'I did, my love. And I bet the boss did, too. You had better be prepared for a call.'

'You are wondering why I haven't been more specific and declared it a murder inquiry?'

'No, I understand why not. That won't be the boss's gripe either. He'll want to know why you agreed to do television before you talked to him.'

The landline phone started to ring. 'Shall I get it, laddie?' Lachlan asked.

Torquil shook his head. 'Sorry, darling,' he said into his mobile. 'You couldn't have been more right. He's on the blower right now, I think. 'Bye.'

He picked up the landline and winced at the torrent of invective that rushed from Superintendent Lumsden's lips.

'And good evening to you, Superintendent,' he replied. 'What exactly can I do for you?'

X

The killer read through the email prior to sending. Although it was only a few words it had been carefully composed.

The message box simply read:

Re THE LATE Dr JANET HORNE

Then the text:

KISMET!
GUESS WHO IS NEXT?
YOU KNOW YOUR CRIMES.
NO ONE CAN ESCAPE THEIR FATE.

A tap on the send button hurled it into cyberspace via the usual method that made it completely untraceable. It went into a black hole, one of the computer servers that randomized emails through an unfathomable maze of cyberspace. Instants later it went into the inbox of the intended victim.

XI

The recipient had been surprised to see an email pop up about Dr Janet Horne. The surprise deepened to disbelief then to shock upon reading it.

But how did anyone know?

The logical thing would be to inform the police. But that was not an option, since there was too much to risk.

7

After finishing the broadcast Murdoch and Gavin had gone back to the Fauld's Hotel where they were staying, for showers and a freshen-up before dining in the restaurant. Then they had gone to the Bonnie Prince Charlie for a leisurely drink before they headed back to the St Ninian's Church tower to prepare to film the next slot in their recording of the *Heavens Above* programme.

The locals had other ideas about it being a leisurely drink, however. They immediately found themselves made the focus of attention of the Bonnie Prince Charlie clientele, many of whom tried to ply them with drinks in an attempt to get inside information on the death of Dr Janet Horne, much as they had tried to do with Calum Steele. When Murdoch adroitly sidestepped their questions they started to lose interest and wandered off to nurse their drinks and find other topics of conversation.

'The folk here are a bit like gannets,' someone said, as they sat at the corner table. 'They'll fly around you until they get what they want.'

They looked up to find a man incongruously dressed in waterproofs, with a baseball cap perched on a large head, standing over them, a pint of Heather Ale in his hand. 'I'm Ming McDonald, one of the local fishermen,' he said, holding out his hand. 'Pleased to meet you both. I am a big fan of *Heavens Above*.'

They shook hands and, without being asked, Ming sat down.

'The thing is,' he went on as he set his pint down on the table, 'I have a theory that I think you as astronomers will be interested in. I think that I have proof for you that this astrology that you take such delight in rubbishing actually has something in it. I have been making an extensive study of the zodiac and planetary movements for a couple of years and I have discovered something that is totally predictable.'

Murdoch smiled benevolently. He was used to such discussions in pubs. 'So you have a telescope, Mr McDonald? What type? A reflector or a refractor.'

'No, no telescope. I just use my ephemeris book that shows me exactly where the planets are and which zodiac sign they are passing through.'

'Ah, you mean an astrological ephemeris, not a proper scientific one?' Murdoch asked.

'That's right, but that is what I am saying. Using it I have been able to predict and prove that astrology works.'

Murdoch smiled thinly. 'Mr McDonald, I am not sure that you are talking to the right folk here. Maybe you should be talking to some of the astrologers who have come to the island. Quite frankly, I am not interested in — '

But Gavin put a hand on his arm. 'Not so hasty, Murdoch. Let's hear what Mr McDonald has to say. It could be something that would make a nice wee feature on *Heavens Above*.'

Murdoch raised a quizzical eyebrow and sat back. Gavin turned to Ming. 'So what is this theory about?'

'It might actually be better if I showed you. Back at my house at Gull's Cove, I have a collection.'

'Er — a collection of what, Mr McDonald?'

'Jellyfish.'

Gavin took a sip of beer and then wiped the foam from his upper lip. 'This sounds fascinating.' He winked at Murdoch. 'We're in, aren't we, Murdoch?'

Murdoch sighed and looked at his watch. 'I suppose so, we have a couple of hours before the conjunction will look at its best, weather permitting.'

Ming McDonald stood up. 'Well, let's go

now. Leave your beer, I may have a drop of something else that's a bit stronger and which will make your time worthwhile.'

He reached into a pocket and took out an unlit cigar which he clamped between his teeth. He grinned. 'I predict it!'

II

Calum and Cora had enjoyed a thoroughly romantic candlelit meal in the kitchen of Calum's flat. Calum had surprised Cora somewhat by ordering a vegetarian curry takeaway for them both from the Spice Pot on Constitution Road. It was the island's only Indian restaurant and the proprietor, Ashok Kumar, had been surprised to find Calum order anything other than a lamb vindaloo. They ate it and washed it down with a bottle of chilled Australian Riesling.

'The things a man does for love,' Calum said softly as he reached for her hand across the table.

'Do you mean that, Calum? Do you really love me?'

'I do, Cora. I think you are the bee's knees.'

She giggled. 'You really know how to use words, don't you, boss?'

'I'm only the boss at the *Chronicle*, lassie.

Here we are . . . partners.'

Cora stood up, circled the table and sat on his knee. She took his spectacles off and put them on the table, then wrapped her arms about his neck and kissed him passionately.

'So . . . partner,' she said, moments later, 'I have a proposition to make.'

'A proposition? I was planning something like that myself, Cora.'

She giggled again. 'Oh yes, I think I know what you mean. Is it about where I spend the night?'

Calum swallowed hard and nodded his head vigorously.

'I think I should stay here tonight.'

Calum squeezed her tightly and leaned forward to kiss her again. But she held him back. 'Just a moment, you sexy man. You haven't heard my proposition yet.'

'Go on then, lassie. At the moment I don't think I could refuse you anything.'

'It's work related,' she went on with slight trepidation. 'I know you are the boss and I don't want you to be offended.'

Calum's eyes narrowed. 'I am all ears, Cora.'

'Well, all this business about astrology and the transit started me thinking. Maybe there is something in astrology after all.'

'Are you going all new age on me, Cora?'

'Not really, it is just that perhaps this could be a time of transition.' She took a deep breath before pressing on.

'I know that the *West Uist Chronicle* is a traditional newspaper and that you do a fantastic job and the whole island reads it every Tuesday and Friday. Also, you go to enormous lengths to produce these special editions. It just takes so much time, at least in the production and the distribution.'

'Aye, it is a chain of production, certainly.'

'I appreciate all that, but then something of national importance comes up like this and you are sent into a frenzy to get it out before someone beats you to it on TV.'

'That is all part of the cut and thrust of journalism.'

'But why don't we use the new technology? You are always impressed by my iPhone, or my clicky-box as you like to call it. It has terrific potential.'

'I'm not sure where this is taking us?'

'The Internet. Why don't we produce a digital version of the *West Uist Chronicle* to run in tandem with the paper edition? Just about everyone has a computer these days with Internet access. If we had a digital *Chronicle* we could update it daily, or even several times a day. You could use Facebook, or Twitter, or any social network to drive people to the *Chronicle* whenever we have serious news. That way we could go national, international, and even global! And we could beat the television every time we had a story.'

Calum stared at her in amazement. 'You really are a genius, Cora. I would just need reassurance that we would only ever act responsibly. I'm prepared to embrace new technology, and you'll have to guide me, but we would never do anything illegal. No tapping phones, no hacking into email accounts, just good, traditional journalism.'

She kissed his nose. 'Of course not! You are the boss.'

'I'm not so sure of that any more,' he whispered as she closed her mouth over his.

'Now back to *your* proposition, lover,' Cora whispered in his ear. 'I am putty in your hands!'

III

Murdoch and Gavin returned from Ming McDonald's place at Gull Cove and ascended the church tower in good time to record a piece about the conjunction of Jupiter and Uranus.

'What did you make of Ming McDonald's theory?' Gavin asked, as he started to pack up his camera equipment afterwards.

'I thought he was an interesting chap. A bit odd, but quite interesting.'

'Did you think there was anything in this theory of his?'

Murdoch laughed. 'About the planets influencing the movements of jellyfish, especially when they pass through the water signs of the zodiac? Come on, Gavin, you cannot be serious. That is utterly bananas.'

'And yet he has charted his catches of the different types of jellyfish. If his figures are to be believed there does seem to have been a correlation. And you have to admit, all those different tanks of jellyfish, all labelled, look very impressive.'

'As I said, he was interesting. But you know as well as I do that unsubstantiated research cannot be relied upon. Scientific fraud is a huge problem in academe, let alone among folk with a quasi-interest in science. As for all that footage you took of his jellyfish tanks, we couldn't possibly use it on the show. It would be cruel to him and he would just come across as eccentric, to say the least. And what do you think it would do for our credibility as a science programme?'

'His house was interesting, didn't you think? He kept it quite neatly. Neater than I would have expected of a bachelor fisherman.'

'What did you expect?' Murdoch returned with a grin. 'Fish heads in the bath, nets all over the place?'

'Well, how do you suggest that we let him down gently?'

'I'll have a word with him before we leave the island.'

Gavin hoisted the bag and slipped the strap over his shoulder. 'Actually, I could tell him that we couldn't use it on *Heavens Above*, if you like?'

Murdoch opened the tower door and held it open for him. He patted his shoulder. 'You splendid fellow, Gavin. You have just given yourself a job.'

'You see, I think I see a bit of potential here, for a short documentary film. I may do a bit more work with him.'

'You are not getting tempted to the other side, are you, Gavin? All this astrology nonsense isn't getting to you, is it?'

Gavin laughed. 'I could have predicted you would have said that! Maybe I'm just more open-minded than you, you old bigot.'

'Gullible, you mean. Well if you find there is something in all that, I'll cook some of those jellyfish for you.'

'Ha! I didn't know you knew anything about Japanese cuisine.'

Murdoch closed the door behind him and

followed the cameraman down the stairs. 'Aye, well, there is maybe a lot that you don't know about me, Gavin, my lad.'

IV

Jerome Morton and Henry Dodds had spent too much time together that day. Normally, Henry would act as the buffer between Rosie and Jerome. He considered that to be part of his role as their agent. Yet with Rosie spending all the time she could with Douglas Drummond, Jerome had become more irritable than ever.

The work they had done that afternoon on the book project had not gone well. Nor had Jerome appreciated Henry's making an idiot of himself at the chandlery with Dr Mathieson. It had embarrassed Jerome and he had told his agent so in no uncertain terms when they had left. The fact that Tam MacOnachie had proved so unhelpful had merely stoked the fires of his ire.

They had dined together at the hotel then gone for a drink at the Bonnie Prince Charlie and, thanks to too much Heather Ale and several whisky chasers, they had argued very publicly.

'You are the most useless agent in the

industry!' Jerome exclaimed.

'And you are the rudest author I have ever worked with. If it hadn't been for Rosie I would never have taken you on as a client. She and I have carried you.'

'You've carried me!'

'I have. You're a talentless writer. You are just a hack.'

'Well, Mr high and mighty Henry Dodds, you can just sod off. You are fired.'

'Fine! You are fired too!'

Blows were only averted by Angus Laird, one of the bar staff, getting between them and frog-marching them both out of the door.

Glowering at each other, they departed in opposite directions along Harbour Street.

V

For some reason Lachlan was unable to sleep that night. Accordingly, rather than lying tossing and turning, he did what he always did on such occasions: he got up, put on his dressing-gown and went down to his study to jot down some ideas for a future sermon. He reasoned that if the Lord didn't want him to sleep, then he probably wanted him to do something useful.

'So, Lord, what message do you think I

should give to our flock on Sunday?'

He sat down at his desk, filled his pipe and began to smoke.

No idea presented itself immediately to him.

'But I suppose there is a question that I should be able to put to you, Lord,' he mused, as he leaned back and watched the smoke curling upwards to the ceiling. 'With this tragic death, which I am going to talk about of course, people will be wondering about the difference between astronomy and astrology. I mean, they both rubbish each other, yet they both have the same origin. They both consider the heavens as their domain.

'Look at my old friend Murdoch Jamieson, *Heavens Above*, for example. He is an out-and-out atheist and he won't even consider that the heavenly bodies could have any predictive effect on life here on earth. And yet, he obviously had some sort of relationship with poor Dr Janet Horne. There seemed to be bitterness between them, as if they had at one time been closer. Maybe they had even had a relationship and it had gone sour. A love-hate relationship, like so many. That's another thing I'll maybe see if I can find out from Murdoch.'

He put his smouldering pipe down in the big ashtray on his desk, cracked his fingers and settled down over his old portable typewriter, which he always kept with paper installed and at the ready.

'Thank you, Lord, if that was your idea. If it wasn't, then it will still do. I am going to talk about things like astronomy and astrology, phrenology and psychology, orthodox and complementary medicine. They all have their proponents and their opponents. Love and hate, the two sides of the coin.'

An idea came to him and he stood up and went to the large floor to ceiling bookcase that was crammed with books on theology, philosophy, golf and a myriad other things that interested his mercurial, but ever-enquiring mind. After a few minutes' search he came back to his desk with an old philosophy book. He propped it open by the side of the typewriter and with a smile of satisfaction began to type:

As the great seventeenth-century Dutch philosopher Baruch Spinoza once said, 'Jealousy is a mixture of love and hate.'

He picked up his pipe and struck a light to it. 'That will do. That is the way I'll start. I'll have a coin ready on the lectern in the pulpit. I'll talk about the two sides of a coin and say how separate they seem, yet when I spin them, they both are seen at the same time. They merge to create a composite of the two.

Thus with Spinoza's idea of love and hate coming together to become jealousy.'

He sat puffing away meditatively for a few moments. 'Yes, love, hate and jealousy: three linked emotions that can have the most tragic of consequences.'

VI

At sunrise the little group of four women finished their vigil at the Sentinel Stone. They had sat or lay down, each taking one side of the monolith as their area to contemplate. They had not talked throughout the whole night.

'Did you all feel her presence?' Iona asked, after they had had a group hug.

'Of course,' said Nettie. 'She and I just sat and comforted each other.'

'I felt confusion,' said Agnes. 'I think she was surprised to find herself on the other side.'

'I felt that she was angry,' Melissa said. 'Her spirit body felt violated about being separated from her physical self. It bodes ill for whoever was responsible for her death. She will haunt them until their own death.'

Nettie looked at her in horror. 'Did you really get that impression? She didn't give me anything so intense.'

Melissa nodded. 'Very distinctly. In fact, I felt quite uncomfortable with her anger.'

Iona adjusted her headband and pursed her lips thoughtfully. 'Now that you mention it, I have to agree. With all of you, actually. She wanted to assure me that her spirit had survived, yet she was confused about why she had passed over before her time and she was angry about someone.' She shook her head wistfully. 'But I am saddened to think that she is going to tie herself to this earthly realm out of a sense of injustice. As we all know, ghosts are unhappy souls who can get stuck between the realms for centuries.'

'What can we do to help her?' Agnes asked.

'I think we should pray again,' Nettie said.

VII

Annie McConville was well known through-out the Western Isles as a slightly eccentric septuagenarian, who ran an animal sanctuary in Kyleshiffin. She was a small, chirpy lady who was remarkably fit for her age, thanks probably to the amount of exercise that she obtained from walking her dogs. She was seldom seen with less than five dogs at a time, although two of them were really her lieutenant and her sergeant. These two; Zimba, a gentle, handsome German Shepherd and Sheila, a small, white West Highland terrier with a prodigious bark, were exceptionally well trained and never needed a lead. Sheila was the lieutenant who barked out orders to any of the waifs or strays that she happened to be exercising, while Zimba, the sergeant, would nip any insubordination in the bud through his strong presence and example.

As usual, Annie had risen at six in the morning, breakfasted on tea and toast then fed the occupants of her kennels and of the adjoining cattery. By 6.30 she was walking up the hill from Kyleshiffin to the moor. On the way she passed Nettie Grant and her three friends.

'Good morning, ladies,' she greeted them, as the three rescue dogs strained at their leashes with much wagging of tails, which elicited a bark of rebuke from Sheila. 'Have you been on your vigil? I saw you on the news last night. A terrible shame the whole thing has been.'

'Yes, Mrs McConville, we shared the vigil and each of us felt Janet's presence,' Nettie replied.

'Aye,' Annie returned with a smile. 'I have no doubt that you did feel her spirit. I have looked after enough poor dogs and cats to know that the spirit survives after death.'

'It must be so hard for atheists when they lose someone,' Agnes said.

'Sadly, there are so many non-believers these days,' added Melissa.

'Well, ladies,' Annie said, marshalling her dogs, 'I had better be going. I have fourteen dogs under my care at the moment and this is the first outing of the day.'

She set off on one of her regular little circuits, allowing one of the rescue dogs off the lead at a time, trusting to Sheila and Zimba to accompany them and keep them under control.

Returning via the Sentinel Stone she made her way down the edge of the moor and weaved her way in and out of the profusion of gorse bushes that lined the track that would lead back to the main path.

Suddenly the leading dog started to bark furiously and scampered off into the bushes. There was silence for a few moments, and then it started to howl.

'Sheila! Zimba! Go and get him. It is time that he went back on the lead.'

The two dogs set off instantly while Annie came after them with the other two dogs, a dachshund and a timid-looking boxer.

Zimba and Sheila had disappeared into the

gorse bushes, but reappeared moments later, both barking like mad.

'Goodness, what's the matter? Have you found a dead rabbit or something?'

Moments later Annie McConville gasped as she joined the three howling dogs.

Lying on his back was the body of a man. Protruding from the blood-soaked chest was what looked like a long arrow.

8

I

The Padre was busily stirring the porridge pot on the Aga while a couple of oatmeal-covered herrings were sizzling in a pan when Torquil came down to breakfast.

'Will you have toast with your herring this morning?' he asked, as he removed the pot and began ladling the porridge into a couple of bowls.

'Yes please, Uncle,' Torquil replied cheerfully. The mixed aromas had stimulated his appetite.

Then his eye fell on the newspaper propped up against the teapot. 'Ah, I see Calum has produced a special edition of the *Chronicle*. He certainly didn't waste any time getting it out.'

'Aye, it is amazing the way he does it. Pass the salt, would you?'

Torquil was busy reading the paper and absently handed Lachlan the pepperpot.

'Oh! What is he playing at!' Torquil exclaimed. 'Look at this headline.'

He turned the paper for the Padre to see.

THE ZODIAC KILLER BAFFLES POLICE

'I thought you would be peeved by it, especially after your statement on the news.'

'Why does the scunner always have to be so sensationalist? I categorically told him that all we could say was that the death was being treated as suspicious until we had further information. And he has implied that there is an unnecessary delay in getting the post-mortem results. Ralph McLelland will not like that either.'

'I am sure you are right. He will be annoyed, too. But you have to admit it looks highly like murder.'

Torquil scanned the article. 'Goodness me, Cora Melville has written a piece about this Grand Cross that Dr Horne was talking about at her lecture. Then she talks about the Salem witch trials in America in 1692 and links it with another episode in Devon ten years before that. Then with a witch being executed in Dornoch in 1727. Finally, she implies that the old Hag Stone on the moor was a meeting place for witches. Hmm! She doesn't really explain any link between them.'

He tossed the paper down on the table and poured milk over his porridge. 'It is clear that Calum is teaching her his journalistic code. Gloss over the facts and imply what you want the reader to think.'

He started his porridge with less appetite

than he had had when he entered the kitchen a few minutes before.

'I'll have a word with him about jumping the gun with his articles. It stirs up anxiety in the public.'

'But it sells copies of the *Chronicle*. And, as you know only too well, that is what he sees as his life's mission.'

'But he hardly helps us,' Torquil replied sourly. 'Once, just once, it would be good if he would listen to what we say and print that instead of a sarcastic jibe like that one about us being baffled. He's one of my best friends, but sometimes I wish he would — '

His mobile phone went off and he saw Morag's picture flashing at him. She had been the duty officer overnight and for some unaccountable reason he felt a shiver shoot up his spine.

'Morning, Morag, what's the emergency?'

The Padre watched Torquil's expression. He saw the way his jaw dropped and his face paled.

'Right, I'll be there as soon as I can.'

He stowed his phone in his back pocket and stood up. 'Can you look after Crusoe again this morning? I'm afraid that I may have to take everything back that I just said about the *Chronicle*. We've got another body and this time there is no doubt about it being a murder. A man has been shot in the chest with some sort of arrow.'

II

Upon receiving Morag's call Ewan had gone straight to the station. He felt like death warmed up. He had been awake half the night with a raging temperature and his throat felt as if he had swallowed a piece of sandpaper. He had no doubt that his early-morning swim to retrieve the body of Dr Horne had resulted in him picking up a chill of some kind. If Morag's news had been any less urgent he would have considered calling in sick, but with so few staff he knew that it was imperative that he should turn in to man the office.

He could hardly believe it: another death, and this one a definite murder. An as yet unidentified male.

'*Creideamh!* Faith!' he exclaimed. 'I am wondering if it has anything to do with this Grand Cross that they are all talking about?'

III

By the time that Torquil arrived at the Sentinel Stone on the Bullet, Morag had set up poles and the official blue and white crime-scene tape around the area.

Ralph McLelland had also been summoned and had arrived in the Kyleshiffin Cottage Hospital ambulance minutes before him. It was not a purpose-built ambulance, but was in fact a converted camper-van, which had been donated by a former laird of Dunshiffin Castle.

Morag met Torquil as he dismounted from the Bullet and pulled off his goggles and helmet.

'It's that literary agent, Henry Dodds,' she informed him. 'I recognized him as soon as I saw him. Annie McConville found him, as I told you on the phone, but it was the first time she had seen him. She hadn't been at the lecture the other night.'

'Where is she?'

'I let her go after I took a brief statement. She's a tough old bird, as you know, but she was shocked and she was worried about the effect the dead body was having on her dogs. One of them seemed very highly strung and was howling. It was a relief when she took him away.'

'And he had been shot with an arrow, you said.'

'Actually, that was what Annie had told us when she phoned. I hadn't seen the body

166

when I set the wheels in motion and called you. It looks like a spear. You know, from a speargun.'

Torquil nodded and followed her through the gap in a thicket of gorse bushes where they found Dr Ralph McLelland kneeling beside a body that he was examining with gloved hands.

It was Henry Dodds, all right. He was lying on his back, his eyes staring upwards sightlessly, his whole face frozen in an expression that suggested both surprise and agony. He was wearing a jacket and polo shirt, both of which were soaked with blood that had escaped from a chest wound, the cause of which was all too apparent. A spear of about a metre in length was protruding from the left side of his chest.

Ralph looked round when he heard Torquil behind him. 'Did you see Calum Steele's special edition of the *Chronicle?*' He shook his head with displeasure. 'He was a wee scunner when we were at school and he still manages to reach new depths. I'm going to give him a piece of my mind when I see him.'

'I thought you'd feel that,' Torquil replied.

'Ah well. Not much doubt about this one, Torquil,' Ralph said, turning to the body. 'This spear looks to have punctured his heart.'

'Is this where he was killed?'

'I don't think so. It looks as if he was

dragged here. You can see some bloodstaining on the heather over there. I'd say he had been shot and then concealed.'

Torquil knelt down. 'What's that, on that stone by his hand?'

'What stone?' Ralph began.

'This one,' Torquil said, pointing to a stone about the size of an orange. 'It's got something scratched on it.' He leaned closer and frowned.

'Correct me if I'm wrong, but isn't a line with an arrow through it the sign of Sagittarius?'

'That's right, boss,' said Morag. 'Sagittarius, the archer.'

They had not heard the sound of a yellow Lambretta scooter arriving a couple of minutes previously. Nor had they heard Calum Steele and Cora Melville sneak through the police taped-off area.

'Sounds as if we were vindicated, Cora,' Calum said as he appeared beside them. 'It looks as if the zodiac killer has struck again.'

There was a click as Cora took a photograph of the body on her iPhone.

IV

Ewan had just brewed a pot of strong tea and had poured a mug for himself in readiness to wash down a couple of paracetamol to try and ease off the fever and the aches that he was feeling throughout his body, when he received the phone call from an agitated Tam MacOnachie.

'It is an emergency, PC McPhee. I need a police officer here straight away. I have been burgled.'

'Your house, do you mean?'

'No, the chandlery.'

'Has anything been taken?'

'I'm not sure yet. Everything seems to have been thrown all over the place. It's as if some madman has just run amok.'

'Is there any serious damage done?'

'Aye! That kayak that the Barton lassie left me to repair. It's had an axe put through it.'

'Are you sure it's an axe that did the damage?'

'Absolutely. The bloody thing is sticking out of the bottom. Look, PC McPhee, I need someone here pronto, do you understand?'

'I do, Mr MacOnachie. But we have another emergency here and I cannot leave the office. Inspector McKinnon and Sergeant Driscoll are busy on an investigation, so I am going to send you one of our best officers.'

There was a strangled groan from the other end of the phone, then, 'Tell me that you are not serious, PC McPhee? Tell me that you are not going to send one of those Drummond clowns?'

Ewan was feeling quite ill and felt greatly in need of both the paracetamol and the tea. 'As I said, Mr MacOnachie, I'll send one of our best officers. And I have to say that I have absolute confidence in our two special constables, Douglas and Wallace Drummond. I'll send one of them along as soon as I can contact them.'

But as soon as he put the phone down he felt anxious. He was worried in case he couldn't even contact them.

V

The last thing that Torquil had wanted to hear was Calum Steele's voice. He still rankled about the special that he had produced with its lurid and derogatory headline.

Dr Ralph McLelland pre-empted him.

'Well, well, our local investigative journalist. So tell me how you got here so early, Calum? You were — '

'We were already awake and hard at work,' Calum replied cheerfully. 'And then we heard your bell going like billy-o up towards the moor.'

'I see,' Torquil said, sarcastically. 'You've

stooped to ambulance chasing.'

Calum turned to Cora. 'Do you see what I have to put up with, Cora? And these two are supposed to be my best friends.'

'Friends tend to show each other a bit of loyalty, Calum Steele,' Ralph said, as he stood up. 'I read that special of yours and I was not impressed. Not impressed at all.'

Calum squinted at him through his spectacles. 'You weren't? Whyever not? It was a good issue.'

Torquil saw Ralph's cheeks colour and he laid a restraining hand on his arm.

'What Ralph means is that we could do with a bit more support, Calum. You know very well that we have to be professional about cases like this. We didn't have enough evidence to categorically state that we were investigating a murder. Your article jumped the gun and may have started a panic.'

'As well as make us look parochial,' Ralph added. 'What were you thinking of by saying that there was a delay in the post-mortem results? These things are important and have to be done properly.'

'Aye, Ralph, no one knows that better than me. But look, the public needs to know what's going on. Sometimes folk just need a wee kick — '

Ralph clenched his teeth. 'Don't you dare

say another word, Calum Steele.'

Calum had already opened his mouth, but at the determined look in Dr McLelland's eye he decided otherwise.

He turned to Torquil. 'Now come on, lads. We heard what you were saying and we've got the picture of the mark on that stone. It is clear enough, isn't it? And our article is spot on. You clearly have a serial killer on your hands and it all has to do with these astrological signs.'

'Hence our headline about the zodiac killer,' said Cora.

Morag had been quiet until this point. 'Perhaps now is the time that we should — er — maybe work together?'

Torquil nodded. 'You are right, Morag. And so now, Calum, you can report a second body has been found, which the West Uist Police are absolutely sure is a case of murder. They are awaiting formal identification of the body, so no mention of a name until I give you the all-clear to release the information.'

'Agreed!'

'And in the light of this and because of certain findings at the scene of the crime — but again, I don't want you to be too precise — they have begun a murder investigation. They have good reason to believe that the two deaths are linked.'

Calum nodded. 'But we're still going to use the term 'the zodiac killer'.'

'OK. But don't use that photograph. Not yet. If there is a serial killer we don't want to feed the twisted ego of a psychopath.'

'I'll use journalistic discretion and treat it properly.' Calum smiled. 'Right then, lads. Are we all friends again? We'll liaise with you later. But right now we've got work to do. Come on, Cora.'

As they left the gorse thicket and made their way back to Calum's Lambretta Cora whispered to him, 'Aren't we going to use that picture, Calum?'

'Not yet, lassie. Like Morag Driscoll said, we want to work with them. Except that it does make sense to announce that they found that Sagittarius symbol, because it really justifies the name of the zodiac killer. The special edition will whet people's appetites and so they will be ready for the next main one. But we've got a bit of a headstart on them.'

'What do you mean, a headstart?'

'We're going to investigate this case and find the murderer ourselves.'

Cora gave a nervous laugh. 'Ooh, real investigative journalism. It sounds a bit — er — risky.'

Calum slid his arm about her shoulders.

'I'll protect you, my love.' He kissed her on the cheek. 'Now, you've also got another important job to do. How quickly can we get the digital issue up and running?'

Cora smiled with enthusiasm. 'A couple of hours. The main thing is having a mailing list to drive people to it for a start with an email. Then Twitter and Facebook.'

'Well, I have a huge email address book. I save everybody's address when they email me. At some stage or another I have probably communicated with every household on the island.'

He clapped his hands with glee and mounted the scooter, then waited for Cora to get on behind him. She squeezed his tummy through his yellow anorak.

'Twenty-first century, here we come.'

VI

Tam MacOnachie was surprised to see both Drummond twins get out of their dilapidated old jeep outside the chandlery.

'I thought that Ewan McPhee was going to send just one of you?' he said, without enthusiasm.

'Well you've got the two of us, which means twice as much efficiency. We hear that

174

you've had a break-in, Egg — I er, mean, Mr MacOnachie?' said Wallace.

'Ewan McPhee couldn't tell us anything other than that you had been burgled,' Douglas explained. 'There has been an emergency and he just told us to come here as quick as we could and investigate.'

The harbour master gave him a sour look. 'Aye, well I have been broken into and whoever did it went to town with an axe. Just look.'

The Drummond twins entered and stood staring about. Douglas whistled.

'Sure, it is the work of a madman that we are seeing here.'

'That girlfriend of yours will not be happy about her kayak being hacked to bits,' Tam said, pointing to the ruined kayak with the axe still sticking out.

'Do you recognize the axe?'

'It is part of my stock. The swine just pulled it out of the rack over there.'

'Has anything else been taken?'

'I am not entirely sure. I haven't made an inventory of the goods. I knew that you lot would want to take pictures and all that.'

'And so we will. But does anything particularly stand out? The cash register? A safe?'

Tam shook his head. 'It doesn't look like he was after money. It looks like wanton damage,' he said, scanning the scattered goods. Then his eye fell on a corner of the shop and he snapped his fingers.

'Well, there is something that has certainly been taken: a speargun.'

Wallace had begun to make notes in a small pocketbook when his mobile phone went off. He answered it and listened to Ewan McPhee's message, his eyes open wide in surprise.

'Right, we'll finish up here and then go and see if he can bring one or other of them in.' He replaced his phone in his pocket and signalled to Douglas.

'Ewan has another job for us, Brother. Just step outside for a moment will you.'

Douglas followed him outside. 'What's the mystery, Wallace?'

'There's been another death. That's the emergency Ewan was talking about. It is a definite murder this time. He wants us to go and get either Rosie or that Jerome bloke. They are needed to identify the body. It looks as though somebody has shot Henry Dodds up on the moor.'

'Shot him?' Douglas gasped. 'What with? A shotgun?'

Wallace shook his head and looked back at the chandlery door to ensure that Eggy MacOnachie had not been listening.

'He was shot with a speargun!'

9

I

Conn MacVicar had been busy with his portering duties at the cottage hospital when he had taken the call from Dr McLelland. He had quickly gone to the mortuary and prepared everything to receive the body prior to a formal identification.

It was never a pleasant business, but he always ensured that a body was as presentable as possible and that the plastic sheet was secured so that there would be no shock exposure of the corpse. The last thing he wanted was to have a relative or friend of the deceased faint in his mortuary room.

Inspector McKinnon and Ralph McLelland had arrived at the same time and Ralph had explained that he had removed the spear, which Sergeant Driscoll had bagged up.

Conn wheeled the trolley out to the ambulance and with help from Ralph transferred the body-bagged corpse to the mortuary. Ralph and Torquil left him to

177

prepare the body for the viewing.

They were waiting in the mortuary office when they heard the Drummond twins' jeep pull up in the car-park. A few moments later they came in with a shocked and somewhat distressed-looking Rosie Barton.

'I am so sorry to ask you to come in under these horrific circumstances, Miss Barton,' Torquil said. 'As I am sure that my special constables will have told you, we were notified this morning about the discovery of the body of a man up on Kyleshiffin Moor. We believe that it is Henry Dodds, but we do need to have a formal identification made.'

Rosie nodded. 'I understand. I just hope it isn't . . . You know what I mean.'

Douglas gave her arm a squeeze and, with a shrug of resignation, she followed Torquil and Ralph through to the viewing room where the outline of the body was visible beneath a green plastic sheet.

'I've seen plenty of ghosts, but never a real dead body,' Rosie said, with a shiver. She nodded to Ralph, who pulled back the sheet to reveal the face.

Rosie gasped and put both hands up to cover her mouth.

'That's my poor Henry all right. What have they done to you?'

II

Torquil called Superintendent Lumsden and was surprised when he answered the phone himself.

'Of course Sgt Golspie isn't here, that's why I answered it. I was wondering where she was myself. Slipshod she has been, ever since she worked on West Uist.'

'Actually, it was you I wanted to talk to, Superintendent. We had a definite murder here this morning. I have no doubt now that we have a serial killer on our hands.'

Torquil expected a tsunami of bile to cascade down the phone at him, but instead his superior officer remained relatively calm. They went through the procedures to follow and the arrangements that Torquil had already made for the investigation.

'Right, you will keep me informed of progress every afternoon. I want to know before each news bulletin.'

'That's what I was planning, sir.'

'Good. And you're going to need more manpower. I'll send Sgt Golspie back to you. She'll be there on the next ferry.'

Torquil could barely conceal the smile at the thought of Lorna working with him again. 'Thank you, sir. I can certainly use the help.'

'I know that, McKinnon. Don't I bloody well know it!'

III

Douglas drove Rosie back to the Masonic Arms Hotel and held the front door open for her.

'Are you sure you'll be OK? You've had a hell of a shock.'

She squeezed his hand and kissed his cheek. 'I'll be fine.'

'I wish I could stay with you for a while, but . . . '

'I know, you are needed at the station. I entirely understand.'

'You must hate this island.'

'I told you, Douglas, you have made this island very appealing to me.' She sighed. 'But this . . . this senseless murder of Henry. It changes things.'

Douglas looked downwards, his face crestfallen. 'I know.'

But then he held her arms and stared her straight in the eyes. 'I promise you we'll get the bastard who did this. Then maybe we can see about us.'

Rosie sighed. 'I agree. But first things first. I had better tell Jerome. He's going to be devastated.'

So preoccupied were they that neither of them had heard the door open.

'I seem to be making a habit of meeting you two canoodling outside this hotel,' said Jerome Morton. 'I heard you mention my name. What am I going to be devastated about?'

Rosie bit her lip and opened her mouth to tell him, but instead she saw the man standing a pace behind Jerome. 'What does he want?' she asked.

Murdoch Jamieson forced a smile, 'Actually, I came to . . . to . . . '

'He came to see you, Rosie. But since you had done a runner, he and I were going to go to that café and he's going to treat me to a slap-up fry-up. Best thing ever for a — '

'Henry has been murdered!' Rosie cut him off. 'Last night, or sometime this morning, someone shot him with some sort of speargun.'

'You cannot be serious?' Jerome gasped.

Douglas intervened. 'I can confirm that. His body was found on Kyleshiffin Moor and we are now conducting a murder investigation.'

'But . . . but . . . he was OK last night,' Jerome jabbered.

'I am so desperately sorry,' said Murdoch. 'Please accept — '

181

'Nothing, Murdoch Jamieson, I accept nothing from you. Now, if you'll all excuse me, I need to lie down.'

And without another word she forced her way between Jerome and Murdoch and entered the hotel.

Douglas wanted to follow her, but deemed it to be both unprofessional and inappropriate in the circumstances.

IV

It was just after ten o'clock when Gavin McIntyre parked the Star Wagon in the back of the Fauld's Hotel car-park and hauled out his equipment. He heard the scrunch of footsteps on the gravel and turned to see Murdoch advancing towards him.

'Wait till you hear what I've got,' he said with a grin.

'Where the hell have you been, Gavin? I told you that I needed the wagon this morning.' And then, before Gavin could reply, 'I take it you know the worst?'

'The worst what?'

Murdoch frowned. 'The worst bloody news: Henry Dodds was found murdered this morning.'

'Murdered? How? Where?'

'He was found on the moor, shot with a speargun.'

'Bloody hell! This place is getting to be a regular slaughter-ground.'

'But that's not all.'

Gavin eyed him quizzically.

'There could be some fallout. I tried to see Rosie Barton about that other matter, and that's when I heard about Dodds's murder.'

'That's not a problem, though, is it?'

'It depends how much she makes public. You know how much scandal of any sort can hurt a TV show.'

'Damn it! Can you limit damage somehow?'

'That could be tricky. It depends on how on the ball the police are. One of the Drummond twins was there and it was a pretty messy scene outside the hotel.'

Gavin whistled softly. 'I hate to say it, Murdoch, but you dug yourself into the hole and you're going to have to be the one who gets yourself out of it.' He shook his head. 'I still can't believe I didn't recognise her the other day.'

V

Torquil convened the meeting as soon as Douglas Drummond returned from dropping off Rosie Barton at the Masonic Arms.

Ewan had taken the ping-pong table net down and laid out pads of paper and pencils around it. He had also brewed a couple of large pots of tea and placed them and an array of mugs in readiness in the centre of the table.

'Right, folk,' said Torquil. 'I've been in touch with Superintendent Lumsden and he is sending Lorna back to help us. She should be with us on this evening's ferry.'

There was a chorus of approval, and then Torquil picked up a marker pen and tapped its end on the freshly cleaned whiteboard that they used for planning major tasks and investigations. 'OK, let's make a start and ensure that we get a quick result on these cases.

'It seems pretty clear that we are dealing with two murders, which seem to have been committed by the same person.'

He wrote the name Dr Janet Horne on one side of the board and Henry Dodds on the other. Then he drew a square around each one.

'So what do we know? Let's get the facts down and brainstorm.'

'Doctor Horne was an astrologer,' Morag volunteered. 'She gave a lecture organized by the West Uist Astrological Society at the

184

Duncan Institute two nights ago. Her body was found floating in the harbour yesterday morning and Ewan pulled her out.'

'She had been struck on the back of the head and Eggy MacOnachie found a bloodstained bottle among a pile of creels on the harbour,' Ewan added. 'It has been sent for forensic analysis.'

Torquil added notes to that effect beneath her name. 'And I just had a word with Ralph McLelland. He's done the postmortem examination and in his opinion she was probably dead before she entered the water.'

He added more notes, then: 'And on the harbour wall near the suspected point of entry was a chalked symbol: two wavy lines which looked like the star sign of Aquarius.'

He looked at them all. 'Did she have any known associates on the island?'

'Melissa Mathieson,' said Ewan. 'Or Doctor Mathieson, as she always insists on being called.'

'What is she a doctor of?' Torquil asked. 'Does anyone know?'

When no one offered an answer, he added her name to the board and circled it. Underneath he wrote *aka Dr Mathieson*, and followed it with a big question mark. 'We'll need to find out about that.'

'And there are her friends in the West Uist Astrological Society,' Morag said. 'I think that the committee consists of Nettie Grant, she's always dressed in black and is I think a self-acknowledged witch. Agnes Frazer, a young Goth and Iona Hamblin, that bonny young woman.'

'Aye, she's bonny, right enough,' Wallace said.

Torquil added notes then pointed to Henry Dodds's name. 'He was a literary agent to Rosie Barton.'

Douglas gave an embarrassed cough. 'I've got a bit to add about this, boss. This morning, after I took Rosie back after she had identified the body, there was a bit of a shemozzle between Rosie, Jerome Morton, her co-author, and Murdoch Jamieson. Apparently Murdoch had gone round to talk to Rosie about something, but saw Jerome instead. I think Jerome was hung-over, because Murdoch was going to treat him to a fry-up. At any rate, neither of them knew that Henry Dodds was dead. When Rosie told them they both seemed shocked and Murdoch tried to say something, but Rosie wouldn't listen to anything he said. She said she wouldn't accept anything from him.'

'Did you ask her what she meant?' Morag asked.

'I thought I should leave her. Our — er — relationship hasn't reached the point of such confidences yet.'

'That's right, Torquil,' added Wallace. 'I can confirm that's why we were both available to go round and check out Eggy MacOnachie's place when Ewan sent us. They are not spending the nights together.'

'What's this about Tam MacOnachie? Torquil asked.

Ewan wiped beads of perspiration from his flushed brow. 'Och, I'm sorry, Inspector. I was going to report to you when you came in but you had to talk to Dr McLelland.' He took a deep breath then went on, 'Tam MacOnachie discovered that his chandlery had been broken into. I sent the twins round to investigate. They were in the process of investigating when you called me and told me to get them to bring Rosie Barton or Jerome Morton to identify the body.'

He looked miserably apologetic. 'I . . . I guess that I'm not thinking as clearly as I should be, sir.'

Torquil smiled sympathetically. It was typical of the big islander. Whenever he called Torquil *inspector* or *sir*, he knew that he felt he had done something wrong or had in some way let the side down.

'You are not looking too well, big fellow,' Torquil said. 'I think you should be getting home to bed.'

Ewan looked horrified. He shook his head vigorously. 'No way, sir! Not when we have all this to sort out. You'll have to wrestle me to the floor to get me to leave.'

'I think you're a bit outnumbered, Ewan,' said Wallace with a grin. 'The Western Isles wrestling champion you may be, but me and my brother are not without a move or two, some dirtier than you might be used to, but together with our good inspector here, I think we could handle you.'

Morag took charge. 'That's quite enough, all of you. I agree with Torquil that Ewan ought to be home in bed, but I also know that he would just lie there feeling guilty and useless. I say that we send him over to Dr McLelland to see if there is any medication that will help him and then he just mans the front desk. Let's keep the big darling well.'

Ewan protested, but Torquil ratified Morag's suggestion. 'The decision is made, Ewan. Besides, with Lorna coming back I think we're going to be covered. As soon as we have the investigation board set up you can head off and see Ralph McLelland.'

And without more ado he added the names Rosie Barton and Jerome Morton beside that of Henry Dodds and circled them, adding the words 'co-author' under each.

Nearby Dr Horne's square he wrote

Murdoch Jamieson's name and circled it, adding 'TV personality and astronomer.'

'What's his camerman's name again?' he asked.

Morag consulted her notebook. 'Gavin McIntyre.'

Torquil added his name and circled it.

'Now let's go back to Henry Dodds. He was killed by a spear from an underwater speargun. And beside the body there was a stone with the sign of Sagittarius written on it.'

He added notes and turned to the Drummond twins. 'You know what I'm going to ask, lads. Was there a speargun taken from the chandlery?

Wallace answered. 'There was. And whoever did it seemed to have taken an axe to Rosie Barton's kayak.'

Torquil clicked his tongue. 'Do we know anyone who could have a grudge against Tam?'

Ewan put his hand up. 'There is no love lost between Ming McDonald and Tam MacOnachie,' he said. And he recounted the various encounters and complaints that he had had from Ming McDonald.

Torquil added the name and the notes.

'Right, let's look at the links and see what we have so far.'

And after a few minutes of further brainstorming the board began to look like a veritable spider's web. But they noticed that Torquil had quite deliberately left a gap in the middle of the web. Now he drew a triangle and put a question mark in it.

'So who is this killer?' he asked, tapping the board with the end of his pen. 'For now I'm just going to take a leaf out of Calum Steele's book and call him the zodiac killer.'

Wallace poked his brother in the ribs. 'Hey, Bruv, we'd better watch out. We've already had Aquarius and Sagittarius, let's hope he hasn't got anything planned for Gemini — the twins!'

VI

Calum was amazed at how swiftly Cora had been able to put the *West Uist Chronicle* website together, on which viewers could read the special digital issue. He thought that it looked classy, modern, and yet managed to retain some of the charm of his beloved newspaper. They had worked on the articles together and both agreed that they had done a great job.

'So now it's time to go live,' Calum said, taking a gulp of sweet coffee laced with a slug of Glen Corlan. 'Send the email, Cora!'

Cora winked at him and then with an elaborate flourish pressed the 'send' button. They watched the cursor spin, then 'email sent' flashed up on the screen.

'Ha, ha!' Calum cried with glee. He put his mug down and gave Cora a big hug and an even bigger kiss on the cheek. 'True brilliance, lassie. The link to the *Chronicle* digital issue has now gone to everyone in my address book. And that is virtually everyone on the island and maybe half of the west coast of Scotland, including Kirstie Macroon at Scottish TV and the editors of several national newspapers.'

Cora brought up the website with the *West Uist Chronicle* logo and a brief introductory sentence announcing that the website would give headline news, but that for fuller coverage readers were advised to consult the usual printed version.

The headline THE ZODIAC KILLER STRIKES TWICE was superimposed on a circular horoscope pattern with the signs of the zodiac running around the outside. Aquarius and Sagittarius stood out in red, underneath which Cora had added a couple of red drops, as if the signs themselves were bleeding.

The lead article had been written by Calum in his purplest of prose.

'It won't be long before the phone starts ringing,' Calum said, rubbing his hands together.

Cora smiled and ran her hands over Calum's shoulders. 'And the next step is to add a *West Uist Chronicle* podcast. Effectively, it would be just like having our own TV station. You can put up special video reports at any time of the day or night. Then just zap the mailbox and all your potential readers will be notified straight away.'

Calum laughed. 'One step at a time, Cora. You have to go gently with me, you know.'

Cora responded with one of her bubbly giggles. 'And how exactly would you like me to be gentle, O Great One?'

Calum grinned as she peeled off his spectacles and tossed them on the desk. 'A good newspaperman is always open to suggestions, Cora.'

VII

By mid-afternoon almost everyone on the island who had a computer had seen the digital issue and reacted in one way or another. Many readers were fascinated. Many others were alarmed and a number were seriously frightened.

The murderer's reaction was not rapid; it was considered. The email was duly composed and prepared for sending through the usual untraceable black hole. It was shorter than the last one.

It simply read:

YOU'RE NEXT!

A tap of the finger sent the fateful message into cyberspace.

The zodiac sign had already been chosen.

10

The evening ferry docked at Kyleshiffin at 6.25 and Sgt Lorna Golspie was the first of the pedestrian passengers to disembark. Torquil and Crusoe were waiting for her. Dressed in a smart pin-striped trouser suit which she usually wore for work, Lorna was twenty-seven and looked the model of efficiency. She was pretty with a pert nose, hazel eyes and Titian locks that tumbled to her shoulders.

'Welcome home, darling,' Torquil said as he hugged and kissed her. 'I just wish it had been under better circumstances than because of a double murder.'

'I know! You can bet that Superintendent Lumsden's reason for sending me back is because he expects us to fail to catch the murderer, so he can indicate that we are both incompetent.' She hugged him back and kissed his nose. 'So we have no alternative but to prove him wrong.'

Crusoe was wagging his tail madly at their feet, but had been trained well enough to know that jumping up at Lorna was not an option. He whimpered, then renewed his tail-wagging as he vigorously licked Lorna's hand when she bent down to stroke and pat him.

'How is Ewan doing? You don't want him to come down with pneumonia.'

'Doctor McLelland gave him an antibiotic today, which seems to have started working remarkably quickly. I guess he's happy that he can stay at work, so it has perked him up.'

He hoisted her backpack onto one shoulder and they joined the stream of people walking along the harbour. They passed the taped-off creels.

'That's where we found the bottle,' he explained. 'I'll bring you up to speed in the morning, but right now I guess you are ready to eat.'

'I'll say. I've been hallucinating about a plate of the Padre's fish pie and a glass of white wine all the way over.'

Torquil laughed. 'And you will be pleased to know that is exactly what awaits you at the manse. Let's hope that you can predict how and when we are going to catch this murderer with equal ease.'

II

Ming McDonald was making plans as to where to lay his creels on the morrow.

He had seen the *Chronicle* digital issue with its headlined article about the zodiac killer. That had whetted his appetite and he had watched both the six o'clock news and then the late evening news as well.

'Ach, that imbecile Tam MacOnachie has had far more exposure than he deserves, the great lummox! And now he's had his shop broken into and trashed.' He screwed up his face and gave a mock babyish cry. 'Boo hoo! Will the poor man have to have his shop mended?'

He struck a match vigorously and applied the flame to his cigar. He puffed it alight and then extinguished the match as he blew out a stream of smoke. 'As if I cared a jot!'

He reached for the ephemeris on the shelf above his desk. He opened it to the date and ran his finger along the list of planets and the zodiacal signs that they were passing through.

'Just as I thought,' he mused as he turned on his computer and keyed in his password. 'It will soon be time to kick arse.'

But then, as soon as he thought it, he felt a pang of doubt; a stab of conscience that sent his mind into overdrive.

'I know what I need to do and who to see next.'

He started to laugh. 'And I know exactly what to take!'

III

Over an early breakfast the next morning prepared by the Padre, Lachlan listened as Lorna quizzed Torquil about the case. The conversation prompted him to mention the question that had been in the back of his mind for a day or two.

'I had been meaning to ask Murdoch when I next saw him, but in view of the fact that you are now conducting a murder investigation maybe I had better leave it up to you. On the night of Dr Horne's lecture, Murdoch had a bit of a confrontation with that Rosie Barton. She said something about academic credibility. I wondered what that was all about.'

'You are right, Lachlan, you had better leave that to us. In fact, we need to know more about Murdoch's previous dealings with Dr Horne as well. There seemed to be friction between the two of them the morning that the kayakers were rescued.'

After breakfast Lorna and Torquil went to work separately. Torquil took Crusoe on his Bullet while Lorna drove her Mini, which she left permanently on West Uist.

Ewan was already in and had the inquiry room all prepared for them. The kettle was just coming to the boil when they arrived and he busied himself infusing the tea while

Torquil familiarized Lorna with the investigation board.

Morag came in shortly afterwards with a bag of butteries from Gordon Allardyce.

Soon, it seemed as if Lorna had never left and they felt that the team had re-established itself. And, as he had accustomed himself to, Crusoe enjoyed being made a fuss of by everyone before scuttling through and curling up in his basket in Torquil's office.

When the Drummond twins arrived, smelling of the sea and fish, and they too had welcomed Lorna back into the fold, Torquil called the team to order.

'Right, guys, I have brought Lorna up to speed and it is time to divvy up tasks. Let's get this case solved as quickly as possible and get the devil responsible put behind bars.'

He pointed to the whiteboard with its web-like arrangement of murder victims and associates, with all the additional notes and with the photographs of the crime scenes, the bodies and the various articles that seemed to appertain to them, which Morag and Ewan had added.

'Just about everyone on this board seems to have links with one or both of the two victims, so we are each going to investigate and interview them. This morning the Padre told Lorna and me about something he had noticed when Murdoch Jamieson attended Dr Horne's lecture the night before she was found in the harbour. It seemed that he and she had some sort of history.'

He added a note to that effect on the board.

'That fits with the scene on the harbour after the kayakers were rescued. They definitely seemed to know each other and there was friction between them.'

Morag nodded her head. 'That's right. I remember. She seemed to be saying that he had a huge ego, or something like that. It was quite an unpleasant meeting.'

Douglas beamed. 'I'll interview Rosie, if you want, boss?'

Torquil shook his head. 'I'm afraid not, Douglas. You are . . . involved with her. I think it would make sense for Lorna to have a chat with Rosie Barton and for Wallace to interview her colleague, Jerome Morton.'

Douglas gave a snort of displeasure, for which he was rebuked by his brother. Then, seeing the sense in Torquil's decision he sat back and folded his arms resignedly.

'Morag, I want you to interview Tam MacOnachie. You have already had a chat with him when you did the forensics on that bottle, but I want to know as much as possible about that break-in.'

Morag sipped her tea. 'Anything specific

that you want to know about, Torquil?'

'The speargun and Rosie Barton's kayak. Why was that targeted?'

He looked at Wallace. 'And I want you to ask Jerome Morton about the buoys at the Cruadalach Isles. It all seems a bit fishy.'

He nodded at Morag. 'And see what Tam thinks on that subject, too. He went out there to put new ones up. Which leaves me to interview Murdoch and his assistant, Gavin McIntyre.'

Ewan looked crestfallen. 'So — er — you just want me to man the fort, sir? Couldn't I do something more useful?'

Torquil smiled. 'As a matter of fact, since you are looking so much better, Ewan, there is something that you can do.'

Ewan's face lit up.

'I would like you to interview the committee of the West Uist Astrological Society.'

Ewan's jaw dropped slightly. 'Of course, Inspector. It will be my pleasure.'

But his expression indicated that he felt it would be far from a pleasure.

IV

Calum and Cora were having a breakfast meeting in bed.

'You know, Cora, I never thought that I was the sort of lad that would appreciate champagne and Rice Krispies, but I have to admit it stimulates the creative juices.'

Cora giggled. 'Oh, I don't know, boss. I think that creativity is your strong suit, if you know what I mean.'

Despite himself, Calum felt himself blush. He took a spoonful of the Rice Krispies from the bowl that rested between them in a hollow of the duvet and then took a good sip from the champagne flute. Instantly he felt the Krispies crackle in his mouth as they absorbed the champagne, then he experienced the delightful little explosion that threw the champagne onto his palate and caused his mind to flood with all sorts of decadent imagery. He was at once a nineteenth-century Parisian *bon viveur*, an ancient Roman hedonist and a modern-day Russian plutocrat.

But most of all, he was a man in love.

'Cora, you are a genius.'

'In what way, lover?'

He loved the way she used that word, yet the prudish part of him always tended to make him fluster and bluster.

'J-Journalistically, I m-mean. You have put your finger on the solution. This killing spree is all about the antipathy of one group towards the other. The astrologers and the astronomers, that is. All we have to do to solve this crime is to find the person with the biggest gripe about the two victims and we have found the murderer.'

Cora leaned across and kissed his cheek before nestling down and stroking his abundantly hairy chest.

'So what is our next move, lover — I mean, boss?'

Calum sighed and gently removed her hand from his chest. 'We have to be serious about this, Cora. Remember that we are dealing with murder here. Investigative journalism is always potentially dangerous. Be guided by me and all will be well.'

'I am yours to command, boss.'

'Aye, well I just need to sort it out in my head, I'll tell you as soon as I have worked out the masterplan. One thing is sure, though, in my opinion.'

'What's that?'

'The zodiac killer is going to rue the day he started his shenanigans in the *West Uist Chronicle's* patch.'

V

The Padre had played three holes and then written the first part of his sermon for

Sunday when he heard the doorbell ring. For a moment he wondered why Crusoe had not immediately started barking, but then he remembered that Torquil had taken him to work.

He put his smouldering pipe down in the ashtray on his desk and left the study to answer the door. He was surprised to find Ming McDonald standing in the porch with a bucket in his hand.

'Ah, Padre, I brought you some nice fresh crabs.'

'Ming, how very kind of you. And quite unexpected.'

'Well, I know that you and Inspector McKinnon are partial to a crab. My cousin tells me. He says you often buy them from his stall on Harbour Street.'

'And so I do. How much are they?'

Ming looked shocked. 'No, no! Nothing at all. They are a gift.'

Lachlan was puzzled, but he was also well used to his parishioners calling unexpectedly with the most random of gifts. He was not at all sure why Ming had chosen this day to make his unexpected call bearing gifts, however.

'Actually, I had something on my mind,' Ming volunteered, 'and I hoped that maybe you could help me. It's a sort of spiritual

203

problem. I think I may need a bit of guidance.'

The Padre stood aside and gestured for him to come in. 'That's what I am here for, Ming. I can't guarantee to have the answer, but I'm certainly happy to listen.'

Ming took off his baseball cap and went in. 'What about the crabs, Padre? Shall I put them in your sink? They are still alive, of course.'

For a moment Lachlan felt a tingle in his spine: he had just realized that the crab was the zodiac sign for the constellation of Cancer.

VI

Torquil phoned ahead and arranged to meet Murdoch in his room in Fauld's Hotel.

'This is a devilish task for you, Torquil,' Murdoch said, offering the easy chair in the corner of the room as he sat on the side of his bed.

Torquil sat down and opened his notebook. 'Dreadful, absolutely dreadful, but we will get the murderer. Whoever it is may think that we are just outer-island plodders, but we have one of the highest rates for crimes solved in the whole of the UK.'

'Then whoever committed these crimes had better be careful. You ought to be broadcasting that fact, if you want my opinion.'

'As a matter of fact I do want your opinion, Murdoch,' Torquil replied. 'What exactly do you think of astrology?'

'It is total bunkum!'

'You do not believe that planetary arrangements, transits and this Grand Cross that the astrologers have been talking about could have any effect on us here on earth?'

'Of course not! Transits are important to us astronomers, but not for any of this prophetic mumbo-jumbo that they go on about. As a scientist I have no truck with it at all, which I repeatedly tell people on the *Heavens Above* programme.'

'So what is the importance of these transits?'

'Well, with the solar system planets we can use them to study the conditions on the planets themselves. But the phenomenon of the transit is of inestimable help in determining which stars have planets that could be like ours. We can then get a good idea as to which of those planets could sustain life.'

And he went on to give a thumbnail description of how this was being done continuously, with both amateur and professional astronomers all over the world focusing telescopes on distant stars, looking for disruptions in the light being emitted from them, which would be consistent with planets transiting between them and an observer on Earth.

'Fascinating,' said Torquil. 'Dr Horne was an astrologer, not an astronomer, wasn't she?'

Murdoch stared at Torquil for moment then adjusted his eyepatch. 'She actually had a first in maths and astronomy, then she did a Ph.D. in the history of astronomy. Seemingly, while she was researching the way early astronomers cast horoscopes she became persuaded that there was some truth in their archaic practices.'

'She had quite a reputation, I understand.'

Murdoch shrugged. 'Her doctorate gave her some credibility.'

'You knew her well, didn't you, Murdoch. You were very close once, weren't you?'

Murdoch bent his head and sighed. 'I knew this would come out one day. Well, yes, it is true; we had a relationship some years ago. How did you find that out?'

Torquil had on his best poker face and ignored the question. It had merely been a guess.

'But she was bitter, wasn't she? She certainly showed that when you met after the kayaking accident, but yet at the lecture she was conciliatory even when you challenged her assertion that astronomy and astrology shared the same roots.'

'Yes, she was bitter about a programme I did about the delusory nature of astrology. She took it personally and accused me of putting my career before our relationship.'

'And the relationship ended?'

'More or less.'

'That is ambiguous, Murdoch. What do you mean?'

Murdoch shuffled his right foot back and forth on the carpet. 'It wasn't just that programme; I kind of had a dalliance with another woman. There wasn't anything serious in that relationship, but Janet wouldn't believe it. She threw me out and we went our separate ways.'

'And, of course, your career has been stellar since then — no pun intended.'

Murdoch smiled modestly. 'I have been fortunate.'

'Has it always been simple good fortune? Rosie Barton seemed to imply otherwise.'

Murdoch stood up and strode to the window and looked out. He took a deep breath and then wheeled round to face Torquil. 'You seem intent on dragging up a bit of mud, Inspector McKinnon.'

The use of his title was not wasted on Torquil. He knew that he was getting under the TV presenter's skin. He pressed on unapologetically. 'Murder is the murkiest of crimes, Murdoch, I need to explore any and all connections between the murder victims and anyone else. You have a significant connection with Dr Horne and you have an indirect connection, it seems, with Henry Dodds. That connection seems to be through Rosie Barton and possibly Jerome Morton. Now tell me, what was Rosie Barton referring to when' — he consulted his notebook then resumed — 'when she said something like this: 'Academic credibility? That is interesting coming from a man who has made a career out of stealing his researchers' work'.'

'Goodness, you had taken that in? My compliments, Inspector. Your uncle would be proud of your attention to detail.' He smiled. 'Lachlan was always a man who studied details.'

Torquil refused to be put off his train of questioning. 'What did she mean?'

Murdoch sighed. 'She was a researcher on the programme before she broke through with her paranormal books. She was under the misguided opinion that a researcher somehow owned the research that she did on the programme's behalf. She was peeved when Gavin and I did an episode using her research on Mayan astrological predictions, but instead of showing the predictions in a positive light we showed that there was no mathematical evidence of a correlation and certainly no actual historical evidence that any Mayan prediction was true.' He shrugged. 'Despite that, or maybe because of it, she went off and wrote a book with Jerome Morton based on her research. She was pissed off with us both.'

Torquil jotted down a few notes. 'I will be talking to Gavin McIntyre after I see you. But finally, just tell me, did you know Henry Dodds well?'

'No. I had never met him until I saw him on the harbour that morning.'

VII

Morag found that Tam MacOnachie was in a more flustered state than usual. Whereas he was usually quite officious and more than a little pompous, on this morning he seemed both anxious and almost ingratiating. She interviewed him in the chandlery, which he was getting back into some semblance of order.

'Sergeant Driscoll, I'll help in whatever way I can to assist you in catching this murderer. I am utterly horrified that the monster used my

209

harbour to commit his crime. I don't mind telling you that I am embarrassed about it.'

'Why is that, Mr MacOnachie?' she asked, as she placed her notebook on the shop counter and pulled out her silver ballpoint pen. 'You weren't embarrassed when we found the murder weapon, or when you did that news interview.'

'Aye, well, that was when there was still a question about whether it was murder or not. But now we have two murders and from what I have heard, Henry Dodds was killed with a spear from a speargun. As you know full well, I had a speargun stolen from my chandlery.'

'Where did you hear that a speargun was used?'

'In the Bonnie Prince Charlie, last night. The whole pub and probably the whole island knows about it.'

Morag made a note. She had a good idea that the rumour would have been started by the island's esteemed newspaper editor, Calum Steele. She knew that Torquil would be irritated by the leak, but he wouldn't be at all surprised. Calum was not averse to using any method to boost the sales of the *Chronicle*. And she had to admit that the new digital edition, which she had read after receiving Calum's email, was an inspired idea. She suspected that Cora had at least had a hand in it.

The young reporter impressed her as a bright young woman. They had certainly given some tantalizing information in their articles.

'I have your previous answers about the murder weapon, but have you any other information that could be of use to us?'

She noticed the film of perspiration on his brow and the slight tremor in his hand. He was clearly anxious.

Tam shook his head. 'No, nothing at all.'

'Any idea why the kayak was hacked to bits with an axe?'

'Search me.'

Morag made more notes, then, 'Well, there is another question that has been bothering us. It's about the buoys out at the Cruadalach Isles. You went out to set up new ones.'

'I did, and I saw the Drummonds out there, taking photographs. It is a disgrace that Trinity House have still not seen fit to have proper sea-bed tied Isolated Danger Mark buoys put down there.'

'Well, perhaps all of this will be enough to get things moving. But we think those buoys were cut deliberately. What do you think?'

'I think that is probably the case, yes.'

'And do you have any idea of anyone who could have done such a thing?'

Tam MacOnachie shook his head emphatically. 'I am afraid that I do not, Sgt Driscoll.'

Morag noted that the perspiration on his brow was even more obvious. She did not believe him. She wondered if he was afraid of something.

VIII

Ewan had telephoned Dr Mathieson and explained that he wanted to meet her and her fellow committee members of the Astrological Society in order to ask them a few questions about the deaths of Dr Horne and Henry Dodds.

She arranged to meet him with the other members of the committee at Nettie Grant's house on Blalowan Wynd. Ewan rode there on Nippy and parked outside the pebble-dashed bungalow with its flower boxes in the windows and brightly coloured hanging baskets on each side of the door. Nettie Grant let him in and he followed her through to her sitting room where the other three women were sitting waiting for him. They had left a seat for him on a large, floppy settee covered in big black cushions, each of which had a red embroidered spider's web on it.

Ewan sat down and cast a wondering eye about the room. Although he had been half-expecting it to be unusual, he had not expected it to be quite so bizarre. It would, he thought, make a good set for a witch's house in a Harry Potter film. Lace curtains prevented passers-by from seeing the large, dark pictures of pentagrams, horoscope charts and Celtic goddesses, and the cabinets full of jars and bottles full of coloured powders, liquids and essences.

Nettie Grant sat down beside him and made a strange gesture in front of him. 'Don't worry, PC McPhee; it is a blessing that I have just made over you, not a curse. I can see that you have a bad cold or some sort of infection'

'A blessing? You mean some sort of healing charm?'

'That's right, Constable. I am a Wiccan. A white witch, if you like. You should find that the cold disappears within a day. My charms usually work fast.'

'Ah,' Ewan replied, feeling a little uneasy about having any sort of charm made over him.

'And are you all — er — Wiccans?'

'We are all spiritually aware,' Melissa Mathieson volunteered. 'But we all belong to different traditions. I follow the Egyptian way.'

'I am a pagan,' said Iona Hamblin.

'And I am a bit of all things spooky and spiritual,' added Agnes Frazer. 'I am a Goth.'

Ewan had begun making notes in his book,

partly to occupy his hands, for he was not feeling comfortable surrounded by the four women, especially since he always felt intimidated by Dr Mathieson, for some reason he couldn't put his finger on. And so thinking, he turned to Melissa Mathieson.

'I see. Could I begin by asking what exactly you are a doctor of, Dr Mathieson?'

She smiled. 'I have an honorary doctorate from the Open International Institute of Radionics. I am a radionics, crystal and angel therapist.'

'You mean you see patients?'

'I call them clients. I see some as a clairvoyant and tarot reader at the shop, but I also help others from a distance. They send me a hair sample and I send them healing and sometimes I send them remedies by post.'

'Melissa is quite famous in our sphere, Constable,' Nettie explained. 'She has clients all around the world.'

'Goodness,' replied Ewan, jotting notes. 'That is impressive.'

'We are hoping that you police folk are going to be impressive,' said Iona Hamblin. 'Now that there is a lunatic wandering about the island.'

'If only people had taken the signs more seriously,' Nettie Grant said with a sad shake of her head.

'Do you mean that these planets and zodiac signs caused someone to kill these two people?'

'In a sense, yes,' Nettie replied. 'It is obviously the work of someone who has gone quite mad. And that's what a lunatic is. Someone who goes mad under the influence of the moon.'

'The *Chronicle* has called him the zodiac killer,' Ewan went on. 'Have you any theory about it, any of you?'

Agnes Frazer leaned forward, causing her cleavage to fall provocatively in his direct line of vision. 'There will be more! There have only been two deaths, but there are twelve signs of the zodiac.'

Ewan gulped and studied his notebook for a moment. 'I understand that you held a vigil up at the Sentinel Stone the night after Dr Horne was found dead?'

Iona Hamblin nodded. 'We did and we all felt her presence. Her spirit was with us.'

Ewan hummed. He was unsure how to react to that. 'Did any of you hear or see anything when you were on the moor?'

'You mean, were we aware that the murderer was on the moor?' Nettie Grant asked.

'Aye.'

'No. None of us noticed anything,' she

returned. 'We would hardly have stayed up there if we had. Why, any one of us could have become the next victim!'

'That is what is worrying us,' Ewan replied. 'That's why we are doing all we can to apprehend him.'

Nettie Grant shuddered and stood up. 'All this talk of murder is quite getting to me. What say I make us all a nice cup of tea?'

Ewan smiled and nodded. It would have been impolite to refuse, but he was not too comfortable about drinking tea brewed by a witch.

IX

Wallace Drummond knocked on Jerome Morton's door at the Masonic Arms Hotel. Jerome scowled at him as he opened it, then said, 'Oh, I thought it was the other one. You had better come in.'

Wallace entered and saw the laptop open on his desk, surrounded by screeds of notes and half-open books.

'You've been working, Mr Morton.'

'Well done, Sherlock,' Jerome replied sarcastically. Then, before Wallace could reply, he smiled and waved his hand in dismissal. 'Forgive me, I didn't mean to be rude. It's partly that I can't quite take a policeman seriously when he's dressed like a fisherman, and partly because my agent has just been murdered.'

'You had a good relationship, did you?'

'Brilliant! Henry was my best friend. Apart from Rosie, that is.'

'That isn't the impression that people got at the Bonnie Prince Charlie last night. We had a report from Angus Laird, one of the barmen, that you were both a bit drunk and that you argued and almost had a fight. He had to physically throw you both out. He said he waited and saw you both go your separate ways.'

Jerome slumped down in the chair behind the desk. 'It was no big deal; creative people often have fallings-out. We would have patched it up in the morning, if . . . '

'If he had come back? But he did not come back, did he? He was found up on Kyleshiffin Moor with a spear in his chest.' Wallace sat down on the easy chair. 'So, where did you go after your argument last night?'

'I went for a walk. A long walk along the coast.'

'A walk that took you all night? We checked with the hotel staff and they say that you came in after breakfast. They said that you were bleeding from a graze on your cheek.' He pointed a finger at Jerome Morton's face. 'It looks raw. Was it from a punch?'

'No, it was not,' the writer replied irritably. 'If you must know, I slept on the beach. It was a warm night and anyway, I had a lot of thinking to do. I had to calm down after my argument with Henry. I told you, it had all got out of hand. And I was a bit drunk. I slipped and grazed my cheek.'

'Can you prove any of this?'

'Do I have to?'

'At some stage it is almost certain that you will need to, yes.'

Jerome Morton drummed his fingers on the desk for a few moments, and then he bit his lower lip and leaned forward. 'Look, I have nothing to hide. I would never have harmed a hair on Henry Dodds's head, if that is what you are getting at.'

Wallace gave a half smile. 'You will forgive me for saying, Mr Morton, but you seem to be getting unnecessarily aggressive.'

Jerome Morton's eyes flashed. 'Actually, I do mind you saying that, just as I mind very much you even suggesting that I would harm my agent. More than that, I think I have every right to be cross about your brother swooping my girlfriend away.'

'Your ex-girlfriend, I understand.'

'Yeah! Whatever! So she is my ex-girlfriend, but she is my current writing colleague and I resent the way that she has been so preoccupied. We are supposed to be writing a book.'

Wallace gave him a pensive look. 'Really? I understood that you were actually all on a kayaking holiday and hadn't intended to be staying on the island?'

'Well, there you are wrong. We were intending to arrive in time for the transit and the Grand Cross, and also to attend Dr Horne's lecture.' He frowned. 'That bloody accident simply dropped Rosie into your brother's waiting arms.'

Wallace decided not to pursue that line. Instead, he said, 'When we came to pick you up on the morning of the accident, who noticed the buoys: you or Henry Dodds?'

'That was Henry.'

Wallace nodded. 'And finally, what is the book you are working on going to be called?'

Jerome Morton hesitated for a moment. *Death Written in the Stars.*'

Wallace eyed him quizzically. 'That is an odd title. What is it about?'

'It is a comprehensive investigation that will effectively prove the truth about astrology.'

'That is a tall order, is it not?'

'Not at all! Our research is all backed up with statistics and state of the art analysis. It shows that there are certain celestial events which are definitely associated with an increase in the number of sudden and violent deaths.'

X

Gavin McIntyre was working in his room when Torquil knocked on the door.

'Come in, Inspector, I was just making a few notes on the computer while I waited for you.'

Torquil noted that his desk was covered with camera equipment and all sorts of photographic paraphernalia. A laptop was open on the bedside table beside an assortment of books on science, travel, food and drink and a couple of rather hefty science fiction novels.

'Are you writing a science fiction novel?' Torquil asked, pointing to the books.

'No, just preparing some notes about the next filming session. That will be our last one here.' He gave a rueful grin. 'Did Murdoch tell you about my novels?'

'He did. He speaks very highly of you and said that the success of *Heavens Above* is down to you in large measure.'

'He's a good bloke to be so generous, but I think it is obvious that Murdoch Jamieson's charisma is what has kept the show going for almost thirty years. I have only worked with him for a half-dozen years.'

'But you are clearly good friends.'

'We enjoy a good healthy banter.'

'You share his confidence?'

'I think so, Inspector McKinnon. Do you mind telling me where we are going with this line of questioning?'

Torquil smiled. 'What was Murdoch's relationship with Rosie Barton?'

It was Gavin's turn to smile. 'Ah, I see. They had a brief affair. He may be knocking on a bit, but the ladies all love him.'

'And they had a major falling-out.'

'They did, although I have to admit that I didn't take it all in at the time. You see, I was a bit depressed. Murdoch handled it all and managed to fend off a law suit that she was threatening us, or rather, threatening the show with.'

'Do you mean she was threatening to sue Scottish TV?'

'No, it meant us: Murdoch and me. We own the company that produces *Heavens Above* between us. Murdoch owns sixty per cent and I have forty. Quite frankly, though, I don't think she had any case.'

'What about Jerome Morton and Henry Dodds? Where do they come in?'

'I don't understand. Come in where? Rosie

only started writing with Morton after she left the show. I presume that was when they got Dodds to take them on as their agent.'

'I see. So you had no previous knowledge of either of them. But what about Dr Janet Horne?'

'Ah, you do know that Murdoch was in a relationship with her. He was still in that relationship when he had the fling with Rosie Barton. He's a bit of a hedonist, you see. I don't think he considered he was doing anything wrong cheating on them both. And I guess that we rather did the dirty on Janet Horne by doing a show that rubbished astrology.'

Torquil nodded and stood up. 'Thank you very much, Mr McIntyre, you have been most helpful.'

As he left the hotel and headed towards the parked Bullet he went over in his mind the things he had learned. One thing seemed clear: Murdoch Jamieson's TV image was at variance with the picture of the man that was starting to emerge.

11

I

Lorna met Rosie Barton in the lounge of the Masonic Arms Hotel, which was deserted apart from them.

At a personal level Lorna always considered herself to be a good judge of character. On the other hand, as a professional, she had enough experience to know that successful criminals were highly adept at projecting a character that could conceal the blackest of hearts and the most depraved of spirits. Sitting opposite her and just chatting about her books to break the ice, Lorna felt herself warming to the writer. She imagined that in other circumstances they could become friends.

'I heard all about that kayaking accident that you had; it must have been terrifying.'

Rosie shook her head. 'Not really, we are — or rather, we were, all experienced kayakers. Poor Henry, I still feel that he will walk in that door any moment with a joke on his lips. He was good at keeping Jerome's and my spirits up.'

'You and Jerome were once an item, before you met my colleague?'

'We were. And Douglas and I are not quite an item yet. I thought before this awful thing happened, and I think it more now, we just need to take things slowly.'

'That is always a safe path to take with relationships at the start,' Lorna agreed. 'But you know that the chandlery was broken into and that your kayak was smashed up with an axe. Any idea who would do that, or why?'

'I just assume it was a madman.'

'Do you know of anyone who could have a reason to kill Henry Dodds?'

Rosie shook her head. 'No one. Henry didn't have an enemy in the world, as far as I know.'

'Were you aware that Jerome Morton and Henry were both drunk the night before he was killed and that they were ejected by one of the bar staff at the Bonnie Prince Charlie?'

Rosie nodded. 'Jerome told me. But that is nothing unusual. There were often little tiffs, but they never meant anything. Writers can be a bit histrionic, you know. We can be a bit like actors.'

'I understand that you yourself had two run-ins with Murdoch Jamieson. Once on the harbour on the morning of the accident and the other at Dr Horne's lecture at the Duncan Institute.'

'Murdoch Jamieson is an arsehole!'

Lorna was surprised at the venom behind her statement. There was no attempt to conceal her contempt. No sign that she was playing a part of any sort.

'Why is that?'

'Basically because he slept with me when I was a researcher on the show and then he stole my research and distorted it to make an episode to discredit astrology. I only discovered afterwards that he was in a relationship all the time with Dr Horne.'

'Are you a believer in astrology?'

'Of course! And Jerome and I are writing a book that will prove its predictive potential.'

'Well, I hope that it does very well. I think perhaps people want to believe that life has a purpose and that there are outside influences that make people do things.'

'Which there are! And sometimes the planets and the stars are in such arrangements that they can produce a devastating effect on an individual, or on several individuals. Take these murders, for example. The transit and the Grand Cross brought them and the murderer to this idyllic little island, and it caused the murderer to end the lives of two wonderful people.'

'Was it predictable, do you think?'

Rosie sighed. 'That is the difficulty. It was

predictable that something dire was about to happen — Dr Horne told everyone that at her lecture — but she had no way of knowing that she would be a murder victim herself.'

Lorna jotted down a few notes. Mentally she was revising her initial assessment of Rosie Barton. She was not sure that her beliefs in astrology were rational, which worried her, since if she was not rational in one area of her life she might not be rational in others. And irrational people could sometimes be swayed to commit murder.

II

The Padre had listened to Ming McDonald expound on his theories about the planets and the movements of jellyfish for what seemed like an age. The man was passionate all right, if not a little bit manic, so he felt it was best to let him just talk. Apart from which, he did find some of his ideas to be quite interesting, although perhaps a bit off the wall. Nonetheless, the photographs he showed him of all the tanks of various species of jellyfish somehow made it all seem plausible.

'You paint an interesting picture, Ming,' Lachlan said. 'So what are you going to do with all this?'

'I might be making a TV documentary with Gavin McIntyre.'

'Really? That is fascinating.'

'Aye, he came round to my place the other night and we talked way into the wee hours. He took a lot of photographs and said that he is going to try and persuade Murdoch Jameson to do an episode of *Heavens Above* about it. But he said he had to be diplomatic about it, because Murdoch might think that it smacked of astrology. He has a thing about that, you know!'

'Oh, I do know. He has a problem with all sorts of belief, including belief in the Lord.'

'Aye, well, we have got a bit side-tracked, Padre. It wasn't just that I wanted to talk to you about.'

'I know; you said that you had a spiritual problem and that you might need guidance.'

'It is a matter of conscience, Padre. I think I have been guilty of doing something that I shouldn't have done. It could be quite serious.'

Lachlan noted the sudden change that had come over the fisherman. He had started to perspire visibly and his hands had begun to shake. Then his expression hardened and he looked angry.

'How serious do you mean, Ming?'

Suddenly, Ming McDonald turned and stared at him. 'What do you mean by that?' he snapped. 'Are you trying to trap me? Are you trying to make me say something?'

The Padre tried to placate him. He didn't like the sudden change in his manner and he prepared himself in case the fisherman made any sudden moves. Although he kept himself fit and played golf regularly he was all too aware that he was sixty-four years of age, probably twenty years older than Ming McDonald.

'No! It was a mistake. Just a big mistake me coming here.' He gathered up his photographs and stuffed them in an inside pocket of his waterproof jacket. 'You just enjoy the crabs I brought and forget that I called.'

And without more ado he got up and left.

Lachlan went through to the kitchen and stood for a few moments looking at the crabs crawling over one another in the bottom of the sink. He methodically filled his pipe as he debated with his conscience, then went through to his study and telephoned the Kyleshiffin police station.

He had a duty of confidentiality to his parishioner, but under the present circumstances he felt that he had a duty to alert someone to Ming McDonald's mental state.

III

Calum and Cora had worked hard on the latest edition of the *Chronicle* and spent a couple of hours fielding enquiries from various newspapers and local radio stations about the zodiac killer.

Calum leaned back in his chair and joined his hands behind his head to form a cushion for his head. 'No doubt about it, the digital issue is a rip-roaring success, Cora. And so too will be the next issue of the paper. Now we just need to outdo the police and solve the case and we'll generate not only national but international interest.'

'So?'

'So, as planned, we split up and do our best investigative journalism. But since this is your first serious attempt at it I am going to give you the easiest task.'

Cora moved over, sat on his lap and slid her arms around his neck to trap his hands in hers. She giggled.

'Got you where I want you, Calum. Now I thought you said that it could be dangerous. I like taking risks, you know, but that doesn't sound very risky to me.'

Cora held onto his hands with one of hers and waggled her free hand in front of him. 'Well, tell me, O Powerful One, or

I'm going to tickle you.'

'Cora, don't! You know I can't stand being tickled. I don't want to have to use force, now.'

She sniggered and moved her free hand nearer to his tummy. 'Tell me!'

'OK! OK! Just let my hands go.'

Once she had done so and was sitting demurely he went on. 'Right, we have two factions, the astrologers and the astronomers. There is a zodiac killer who has knocked off two people. We need to flush him out.'

'Or her!'

'Aye, or her. So what we are going to do is go fishing.'

Cora eyed him as if he had gone crazy. 'Fishing?'

'Not literally, lassie, metaphorically. We are going to throw out some bait.'

'I don't follow.'

'We are going to go round the two groups, and let it be known, fairly subtly, that we are about to post an exposure about the killer and that an arrest will follow immediately afterwards. You tackle the astrology crew and I'll take the astronomers.'

'But there are lots of them. How will we ever get round them all?'

'That's journalism, Cora. It sometimes needs a lot of elbow grease.'

'I think it's a great idea, Calum, but it

could be a very time-consuming business, and it may seem very contrived. Why don't we use technology?'

Calum looked doubtful. 'I don't want to overplay our hand with the technology, Cora. There could be a danger that folk will stop buying the newspaper and skim the main news from the digital issue.'

'Actually, I wasn't directly thinking of another digital issue. Don't you think that this is the time for us to do a video podcast? We could do it quickly and alert everyone on the contact list at a set time, like maybe four o'clock. We would be more than likely to reach the killer that way, I think.'

Calum snapped his fingers. 'You are right. We'll video me sitting at the editor's desk. I'll say that we have a good idea of who the killer is and that we'll be announcing it in the next digital issue first thing in the morning. Then I'll say that we will be following that up with an exclusive in the regular paper.'

Cora bit her lip pensively. 'Have we thought this through, though, Calum? Aren't we risking a lot by saying that we're going to unmask the killer when we have no idea at the moment who it is? Won't the police be furious with us?'

'Aye to the first and aye again to the second. It is a bit of a gamble, Cora. We investigative journalists have to be prepared to take risks to get the story.' He grinned and went on, 'Just think of it, Cora. The *West Uist Chronicle* not only solves a double murder, but it catches the murderer. It is a risk, but it is a calculated risk that I firmly believe will pay off.'

It was Cora's turn to look sceptical. 'I'm starting to get a bit worried here. I mean, what exactly do you think will happen?'

Calum's eyes seemed to enlarge behind his wire-framed spectacles. 'Quite simply, my love, the killer will come after us and try to stop us exposing him tomorrow morning.'

IV

Douglas had been less than enamoured at being left out of the investigation, but had followed Torquil's instruction to man the office desk. He answered the Padre's telephone call and noted his concerns down in the duty ledger.

So, Ming McDonald may have finally flipped, he mused to himself as he replaced the receiver on the telephone. I had better let Torquil know straight away.

As it happened, Torquil had returned to pick up Crusoe from his office and take him for a walk up on the moor. He listened as

Douglas recounted the telephone conversation. When he mentioned the crabs that Ming McDonald had left him he decided to call his uncle himself.

'And you think he was a bit disturbed?' he asked, after hearing Lachlan's retelling of the encounter.

'Not at first, but then he seemed to change suddenly. It was a bit alarming, because he is stocky and fit. I'm not sure I would have read too much into it if he hadn't brought me that bucket of crabs, and we hadn't just had two murders attributed to a zodiac killer.

'But he seemed quite focused at the start and was fairly excited when he said that Gavin McIntyre was going to maybe do a documentary with him and try and persuade Murdoch to run an episode of *Heavens Above* on it. Then that sudden mood change almost seemed paranoid. I thought I had better report it.'

'That was exactly the right thing to do, Lachlan. We'll need to check him out and probably get Ralph McLelland to assess his mental state if needed.'

Douglas was hovering at the office door when he came out with Crusoe scampering at his feet.

'Would you like me to take Crusoe for a walk, boss?' he asked.

Torquil grinned. 'Are you getting cabin fever, Douglas?'

'Aye, maybe a wee bit. And I'd like to see Rosie, but at the moment I don't think it would be a good idea.'

'That's true. But I have a job for you and Wallace when he gets back. I'd like you to go and find Ming McDonald. If he is disturbed then I'd like you to hang onto him and then we'll get Ralph McLelland to see him.'

Crusoe wagged his tail and barked enthusiastically.

'OK, boy,' Torquil said, attaching the lead to his collar. Then turning to Douglas, 'I'll just take him for a quick walk. Wallace should be back soon, and then I, or Ewan when he returns, will look after the office. Then I want us all back here for a team meeting at four o'clock. After that I will have the dubious pleasure of briefing Superintendent Lumsden.'

V

The killer was feeling anxious. The situation was getting critical and each passing hour was becoming more dangerous.

The need to appear normal and carry on with the usual tasks was of paramount importance. Yet there were so many uncertainties.

Indeed, only one thing was certain.

There had to be another death soon.

VI

Jerome Morton had gone in search of Rosie
Barton after lunch. He found her down at the
harbour where his and Henry's kayaks had
been hauled up the harbour ramp and
stacked in the rack at the end of the harbour
wall.

'I thought I might find you here,' he said,
as he approached her.

She was sitting next to the kayaks with her
back against the wall and her legs straight out
in front of her. She smiled winsomely. 'I wanted
to be near something of Henry's and his room
is locked while the murder investigation goes
on.'

'I thought you might be with Drummond
at first. I phoned the police station, but someone said that they couldn't divulge where any
of their officers were, but they could confirm
that you weren't at the station. I thought
then that there was a good chance you'd want
to connect with him.'

'That's exactly what I do want to do, Jerome.
I want to try to connect with him. That's
why I came here, to try to see if I could get a

message from being near his kayak. But I can't.'

'You are serious, aren't you?'

'Desperately serious! I want to hold a séance. I want to know how his spirit is.'

Jerome looked at her doubtfully. 'I'm not sure that's a good idea, Rosie.'

'Why not?' she demanded. 'We want to know why he was killed so brutally, don't we?'

'Yes, but — '

'But nothing, Jerome,' Rosie replied. 'I'm going to Dr Mathieson's Candle and Crystal store. She's a clairvoyant and may be able to help.'

Jerome shook his head. 'I'm not so sure that she'd be the best person to help. After all, it was pretty obvious that Henry had a crush on her.'

'Then maybe she can put us in touch with another clairvoyant. I'm serious about this, Jerome. Are you coming with me?'

Jerome scratched his ear for a moment then nodded. 'Sure, Rosie. I'll come.'

VII

Tam MacOnachie had watched Rosie Barton and Jerome Morton through the window of his chandlery and been surprised, but quite relieved that they had not come to see him to

236

check on the state of her kayak. After all, it had been the top end of the range, worth at least three grand, and it had been hacked to bits. After the Drummond twins had come round after the event he had immediately contacted his insurance company and had been horrified to hear that his policy did not include damage caused during a burglary.

'If the kayak had been stolen, that would have been quite a different matter,' the person on the other end of the phone had politely and sympathetically informed him. He had mumbled some words of displeasure to her, put down the phone and then immediately cursed the burglar for simply hacking it instead of stealing the damned thing. And ever since then he had worried about the inevitable confrontation that he would have with Rosie Barton, especially since he suspected that he personally would end up having to stump up the cost of the repairs, or rather of the replacement. Parting with money was not one of Tam MacOnachie's favourite pastimes.

He had gone through to the back of the chandlery to make a cup of tea when he heard the door being thrown open loudly and the sound of heavy boots entering the shop. Then a fist banging repeatedly on the counter.

'Tam MacOnachie, get your arse out here!'

a voice thundered.

'*Creideamh*! Faith!' he whispered in alarm to himself. 'That is all I need. The lunatic!'

He pulled out his mobile phone from his brown shop-coat and quickly called the police.

VIII

Doctor Ralph McLelland responded to Wallace Drummond's phone call straight away. Psychiatry had never been his favourite discipline of medicine, partly because by nature he was more interested in the physical and practical side of the profession. However, as a good doctor he strove to suppress any personal prejudice and always turned out when called.

Besides, he knew and liked Ming McDonald and was both surprised and intrigued when he heard that the police had been called to Tam MacOnachie's chandlery to contain and hold the local fisherman.

'I tell you he is a disgrace!' Ming said, as soon as Ralph attended. 'He calls himself a harbour master, but look what happens. We get a transit and he lets a murderer loose in his harbour! Then he lets someone burgle his shop and steal a speargun to murder someone else. He pays no attention to the stars and planets, or to the movement of the jellyfish, and he expects us all to just let him keep his job. I say he needs to go now.'

'He thinks I am the worst villain on the planet,' Tam MacOnachie said with a shake of his head. 'I have no idea why.'

'And he has been going on like this ever since we arrived fifteen minutes ago,' said Douglas Drummond.

'Torquil got a message from the Padre to say that he had brought him a bucket of crabs and he was going on about the jellyfish and how the stars and planets affected them,' Wallace told him quietly. 'Torquil sent us to find him and assess him and then to ask you to see him if needed.'

'It is the effect of the zodiac,' said Ming McDonald. 'And you can all stop whispering. I know what you are up to.'

IX

Later that afternoon Torquil drew the meeting to order.

'OK then, we all know that Ralph has taken Ming McDonald into the cottage hospital and has sedated him while they wait for a psychiatrist to come over from Lewis. He may need to be sectioned under the Mental Health Act of Scotland. We certainly need to interview him properly as soon as possible.'

'He was as high as a kite,' Douglas said. 'I think poor old Tam MacOnachie was really worried.'

'He had every right to be,' added his brother. 'He looked as if he could have lashed out at any moment. He might have done if we hadn't been there.'

Ewan started pouring tea for everyone.

'Do you think he was responsible for the murders?' Morag asked. 'From what the lads told us it sounds as if he ticks a few boxes. He was not acting rationally. And he seems to have a fixation about the stars and the planets.'

Torquil added notes to the whiteboard.

'Aye, the Padre told me that he has developed a theory about the way that various planetary movements affect the movement of jellyfish. He collects them in big tanks at his cottage. He has all sorts of species there.'

Lorna nodded. 'Also, he has a grudge against Tam MacOnachie.'

Ewan circled with the tea tray.

'He certainly does,' he said. 'He has been coming in here to complain about him an awful lot lately. And don't forget that the bottle used to cosh Dr Horne was found in amongst his creels on the harbour.'

Torquil's mobile phone pinged in his pocket. He pulled it out just as a series of similar pings rang out around the room. All of the others looked at their phones.

'It's a text from Calum,' Torquil said. And he read out the text message that had flashed up on all of their phones.

'Follow the link to watch the West Uist Podcast about the ZODIAC MURDERER — his identity will be released in the digital issue of the *West Uist Chronicle* tomorrow morning.'

'Oh, for goodness sake! Torquil exclaimed. 'What is the stupid wee man up to now?'

He clicked the link and saw a video clip of Calum dressed in his trademark bow-tie and editorial braces.

'Welcome *Chronicle* reader,' Calum said on the clip. He pushed his spectacles back on his nose and leaned towards the camera, his face deadly serious. 'This is just to alert you to the fact that tomorrow morning the digital issue of the *West Uist Chronicle* will unmask the zodiac killer and arrange for his immediate arrest. Then in a special edition of the actual newspaper, which will also be available later, you will be able to read the exclusive

241

news about how our investigative journalists solved the case. Until then, this is the editor, Calum Steele signing off.'

There were gasps of astonishment and a torrent of curses from the twins.

'I don't believe it,' said Torquil. 'He has gone too far this time. This is interfering with a police investigation.'

'Does he really know something that we don't?' Lorna asked. 'Clearly, he doesn't know about Ming McDonald.'

'Well, we don't know whether Ming McDonald is actually responsible either,' said Torquil. He looked at his watch. 'It's just after four o'clock now. I'll go and check out Ming's house and have a look for a speargun. Meanwhile someone needs to go over to the *Chronicle* and wring Calum's neck.'

'I think we need to draw straws for that, boss,' said Morag.

The landline telephone rang and Crusoe's bark sounded out from Torquil's office.

Ewan came back in a moment, his expression one of pained apology. 'Sorry, boss, it is Superintendent Lumsden for you. He sounds angrier than usual.'

Torquil went through to answer the call. He stopped and turned at the door. 'This will be Calum's doing. Whoever does go over to tick him off, just make sure that they tell him

242

that when I next see him I'm going to kick his backside.'

X

The murderer watched the video clip of Calum Steele three times.

So that idiotic man was going to make his revelation in the morning, was he?

Action was called for before then.

There would be a revelation all right.

And an appropriate death.

12

Torquil was still rankling after the lambasting he had received from Superintendent Lumsden, who had gone off at the deep end and threatened him with all sorts of disciplinary action before Torquil finally managed to tell him about Ming McDonald.

'Have you arrested him?' he had snapped.

'Not yet. He is not fit for questioning. Doctor McLelland has sedated him and we are awaiting a formal psychiatric assessment, since he may need to be sectioned.'

'Right, well, in the meanwhile sort out that Calum Steele buffoon. I didn't appreciate him sending me that text message. Just how the hell did he get my phone number anyway?'

'Calum Steele is like a ferret, Superintendent. He can sniff information out of a stone.'

'Well pre-empt the little bleeder. Get onto Scottish TV and tell them that you have made significant progress and that an arrest is imminent. And let them know that there have been unfounded rumours spread by the local press that should not be given credence.'

Torquil made the call to Scottish TV and spoke to Kirstie Macroon herself, being careful of the words that he used, since he was all too aware of how easily things could be misinterpreted.

He rode out to Ming McDonald's cottage at Gull Cove with Crusoe in one of the panniers of the Bullet.

The Drummonds' instructions on how to find the place came in very useful since the house was not visible from the road. To get there he had to take an obscure, winding track off the road that twisted and twined for about 200 yards before it opened up to reveal the house and Gull Cove.

It was an unimposing, whitewashed, two-storeyed house with an overgrown vegetable patch on one side and an outhouse on the other. A ramp led from a path down to a jetty where Ming would sometimes moor his boat. According to the twins that was more often than not of late, owing to his on-going dispute with the harbour master. However, on this occasion he had left it moored in the harbour at Kyleshiffin.

Torquil parked the Bullet and lifted Crusoe out. 'Don't wander too far,' he said, as the dog cheerfully disappeared into the under-growth. 'Ha! Looks like you've caught the smell of something. Go on, then, see if you can catch a rabbit for tea,' he called after him. Then, turning to the house he mused to himself, 'And I'll see if I can sniff out a murder weapon.'

The single back door was unlocked, as most people's doors were on West Uist. He walked in through the kitchen, which was scrupulously clean but which had the unmistakable smell of fried fish about it.

He checked out the sitting room, bathroom and the two bedrooms upstairs, but found nothing that he would not expect to find in an inshore fisherman's house. The walls were bedecked with framed pictures of ships, photographs of his parents and cousins and lots of sea-orientated ornaments.

The outhouse, however, was a revelation. It contained six large plastic tanks full of seawater, each of which contained masses of jellyfish. There were pipes linking them all up and the continuous hum of filtration units and the noise of a pump. Torquil noted the handwritten labels of the various types of jellyfish, each with both Latin names followed by their common names in brackets.

He walked down the line, peering inside and reading the names. *Cyanea capillata* (Lion's Mane), *Pelagia noctiluca* (Portuguese Man o'War), *Aurelia aurita* (Moon jellyfish).

He whistled. 'I am no expert, but he seemed to have been going about this in a quasi-scientific way and it looks as if he is onto something. Some of these are not normally found in our waters. Perhaps he is right, maybe something is causing them to move, although I suspect it is more gobal warming than planetary movements.'

He looked at the office area on the other side of the outhouse, with its neat row of ledgers and books. Beside a computer was a stack of both astronomical and astrological texts.

He leafed through a foolscap notebook and noted Ming's scrawling handwriting, which was at variance with the rows of neatly penned figures. It was almost as if one part of him was quick and impulsive and the other was careful, calculating and methodical.

'You've been at this for some time, haven't you, Ming?' he said to the air. 'It seems to have become an obsession. A dangerous obsession that has maybe tipped you over the edge.'

But after as thorough a search as he could manage Torquil left the outhouse and whistled for Crusoe. A moment later the young dog bounded out of the undergrowth with his tail wagging furiously.

'Looks like you've had fun, but drawn a

blank with rabbits. A bit like me, really. I've had an interesting time, but also drawn a blank. I haven't found a speargun, or anything that really links him to either death.'

II

Lorna and Morag both went to the *Chronicle* offices to confront Calum. They found both him and Cora upstairs hard at work on various articles for the special issue planned for the next day.

'You have really set the cat among the pigeons this time, Calum Steele!' was Morag's opening gambit.

Calum grinned at her. 'I thought someone would call round to congratulate us.'

Lorna stared at him in disbelief for a moment. 'Congratulate you? You're lucky we don't consider throwing the book at you. How ... how irresponsible to send that podcast out.'

'Irresponsible?' Calum repeated in wonder. 'Me? I am the epitome of responsible journalism. I haven't said a word that I don't expect to be able to prove.'

'So you know who this zodiac killer is, do you?' Morag demanded. 'Out with it, then, and we will handle it from here.'

Calum leaned back in his editorial chair and smugly folded his arms. 'I said that I expect to be able to prove what I say; I didn't say that I actually know at this moment.'

'You don't know and you have put that drivel on the web? If that isn't irresponsible, I don't know what is,' said Morag.

'But I will know by morning.'

'How?' Lorna asked.

'Calum!' Cora said with concern.

Morag turned to her. 'I thought that you would have more sense, Cora. This . . . this moron is turning your head.'

'This moron happens to be my boyfriend and my editor, if you don't mind,' Cora replied spiritedly. 'And he is anything but a moron,' she added.

'That is a matter of opinion,' Morag said. And then to Calum, 'So how are you proposing to make this discovery?'

'Ah well, that is the tricky bit. I can't tell you, I am afraid. Journalistic ethics, you see.'

'Journalistic hogwash!' exclaimed Lorna in exasperation. 'Take warning, Calum, we may be back in the morning to give you more than you have planned.'

It was only when they had left the office that Morag reminded Lorna that she had forgotten to deliver Torquil's message.

III

Rather as Torquil suspected, the Scottish TV six o'clock news screened both Calum's video, then Torquil's telephone conversation with Kirstie Macroon.

The Padre had prepared a special meal of crab thermidor with parmesan cheese to mark Lorna's early return and the three of them were having a pre-dinner drink while they watched the news.

'At least you redressed the balance a bit, Torquil,' Lorna said, sipping her sherry.

'Aye, he did, but human nature is such that you'll get a flood of folk tuning in for that digital issue of the *Chronicle* in the morning,' Lachlan said.

He raised his whisky tumbler. 'Well, here's to you both and let's just hope that it turns out that Ming McDonald is your culprit. Or rather, let's hope that the killer is not still on the loose.'

IV

Douglas had been in low spirits all day and although he had thought it best not to see Rosie, yet he could not resist ringing her, just to hear her voice.

He tried phoning several times over an hour and each time was dismayed to find that her voicemail immediately kicked in.

He began to worry about her.

And he began to feel worried in case she and Jerome Morton had somehow rekindled feelings for each other, considering the loss that they had both suffered. Part of him felt it would be a natural force that could make them seek solace in each other's arms.

In fact, at that very moment Rosie and Jerome were holding hands in the moonlight. But they were not alone. They were up at the Sentinel Stone on Kyleshiffin Moor, forming a ring around the megalith with the four committee members of the West Uist Astrological Society. It had been Melissa Mathieson's suggestion that they hold a séance there at dusk when they could see the waning moon.

'It is a splendid idea,' Nettie Grant had agreed. 'The waning moon represents the White Goddess in her crone aspect, when she gives praise to Hecate. It is a perfect time for communicating with the recently departed.'

They were all sitting cross-legged, holding hands with their eyes closed and chanting the word '*aum*'.

Melissa Mathieson explained that the three components of the word represented the outer, inner and super-conscient states of

251

consciousness. By repeating it over and over while thinking of the spirit one wanted to contact, it would open up a gateway between the two realms and allow the departed soul to make contact.

They had no idea how long they had been doing it when Agnes Frazer suddenly began to sob uncontrollably, and then Iona Hamblin screamed out: 'Murder! Murder! Murder!'

Then she fainted and the ring was broken.

V

Murdoch and Gavin had filmed the last sequence for the next *Heavens Above* show from the top of St Ninian's tower.

'I usually feel a bit sad after we've finished a location sequence,' Gavin said as he stowed his equipment into his various bags. 'This has been a real roller-coaster of tragedy upon tragedy.'

'It has indeed. Not to mention a fair bit of exposure of dirty washing. Let's just hope that Rosie doesn't get too embittered and do a hatchet job on us.'

'On you, Murdoch.'

'On us both, my friend! If she agitates enough she could drag a lot of dirt down on the show and maybe even find some smart lawyer who could make life very difficult for us.'

Gavin slapped him on the back. 'I think that you're getting a bit paranoid, old friend. A bit like that Ming McDonald.'

News of the fracas at the chandlery had spread like wildfire around the town and they had heard about it when they stopped by the Bonnie Prince Charlie for a half of Heather Ale before they came out to film the waning moon.

'Did he seem off his head when you saw him last night?'

Gavin shook his head. 'He was a bit odd, but that was all.' He pointed to the crescent-shaped moon. 'I thought it was a full moon when folk went potty.'

Despite himself Murdoch Jamieson shivered. 'Come on, let's get back. What say you to a swift dram at the hotel bar?' He yawned. 'Then it's an early night for me, I think.'

VII

Calum and Cora had ordered a takeaway and had eaten in the *Chronicle* office. Calum had pulled the blinds down and arranged a pile of cushions on a chair and topped them with a football and then positioned it in the window with the light shining on it so that from outside it would look vaguely as if he was sitting by his desk.

'Sherlock Holmes did this in *The Adventure of the Empty House*,' he informed Cora. 'From outside that will look just like me. All we have to do is move it about every now and then.'

Cora shivered. 'You know, Calum, I'm beginning to like this idea less and less. I think it is really dangerous.'

He gave her a hug and then switched off the stair lights.

'I'm here, my love, and I'll take good care of you.' He grinned and added, 'Besides, we have these,' handing her an old wooden-headed golf club as he brandished his old shinty stick. 'Tonight's the night that we're going to catch a murderer.'

VIII

The Padre had gone to bed when the landline rang. Torquil answered it and was surprised to hear Ralph McLelland's voice. His tone was urgent.

'Bad news, I'm afraid, Torquil. Ming McDonald has absconded. He wasn't as sedated as I thought and when Sister Lamb checked on him she found that he'd scarpered. I'm sorry.'

'It's not your fault, Ralph. I'll get the team out and we'll find him and bring him back as soon as possible.'

'There's more, though. Before he went he somehow managed to get into the mortuary. He's taken a dissecting kit.'

'What's in the kit, Ralph?' Torquil asked nervously.

'Some seriously sharp and dangerous knives.'

13

I

The team convened at the station ten minutes later and discussed where they thought Ming would be likely to make for.

'I think he'll head for his boat,' said Wallace.

'I agree,' Douglas added. 'He's a fisherman and the boat is almost a part of him. It is where I would go.'

'On the other hand he might head for home. He might feel safest there,' Morag suggested.

'And don't forget he has a thing about Tam MacOnachie,' Ewan pointed out. 'Maybe we need to warn him and check out his house.'

'Good thinking, Ewan,' said Torquil.

'And let's not forget Calum Steele and Cora Melville,' Lorna said. 'After that podcast they could be a target for him, if he is the killer.'

'Do you think so?' Morag asked. 'After all, he was already sedated in the cottage hospital when they sent that podcast out. He couldn't have known about it. I think they are safe.'

Torquil was looking at the whiteboard with its spider-web of people and associations. He tapped it in some concern.

'But if he is the killer then I may have been stupid in getting us all to come here first. Remember that he went to see my uncle and it was Lachlan who alerted us to his behaviour.'

Lorna put a hand to her mouth. 'Oh gosh! And he brought him those crabs, didn't he? Cancer the crab! He might have unfinished business, and the Padre is in bed.'

'Right! I'm going back home right away,' said Torquil. 'Wallace and Douglas, you go and check out his boat in the harbour. Morag and Lorna, can you check out his house?'

'We can,' replied Morag, 'Except you said it was hard to find. Wouldn't it be better for you to go there, especially when it's dark? The two of us can go and check on the Padre.'

Torquil looked doubtful.

'Crusoe is there, Torquil,' Lorna pointed out. 'If there was anyone trying to break in he'd wake Lachlan.'

Torquil nodded and started for the door.

'I'll ring Tam MacOnachie and the Padre then I'll go round to Tam's house, if that's all right with you, boss?' Ewan asked.

'Good. All good,' said Torquil. 'Go, everyone.'

II

Jerome and Rosie had left the Sentinel Stone once they had made sure that Iona Hamblin had recovered from her faint. The woman had clearly been deeply shaken by her experience, as had Agnes Frazer, yet neither admitted to having had a contact from Henry Dodds's spirit. They arranged to call on them in the morning, when everyone had had the opportunity of a good night's sleep.

'You do know that they are going to have another séance without us at midnight?' Jerome asked, when they reached the door of the Masonic Arms Hotel, the two of them having walked back hand in hand, yet without talking.

'How do you know that?'

'Big ears! I heard them whispering that they would meet at one of their houses as we were walking away. Nettie's house, I think.'

'Jerome, I have been so confused.'

'I know.'

'I think it's been a classic case of — '

'A classic case of jumping out of the frying pan into the fire. That's what I thought, Rosie.'

And they kissed.

'Should we?' Jerome asked when they eventually separated for breath.

She stroked his cheek. 'Let's just take it slowly, shall we? After Henry and everything.

It wouldn't be right.'

'What about *him*?'

Rosie bit her lip. 'I'll tell him in the morning. Now let's both just get a good night's sleep.'

III

The murderer watched the shadowy figure make its way along the dark, deserted street as furtively as possible. It had been both amusing and thrilling to watch without being detected.

But the murderer was even more adept at stealth and waited until the very moment when the figure reached the door and put a hand on the doorhandle before dashing out.

The blow instantly felled the victim, who had been given no time to do anything more than register the presence of the attacker before feeling an explosive pain in the head then a sudden lapse into deep unconsciousness.

A smile hovered over cruel lips.

'Soon, there will be another zodiac murder.'

IV

Wallace and Douglas arrived at the harbour and made their way down the steps and along the quay to Ming McDonald's boat.

'Be careful, Douglas. If he's on there and he has blades . . . '

'You be careful, too, big Brother.'

They grinned at each other in the faint moonlight as Douglas climbed aboard.

Almost immediately, he slipped and fell.

'What the hell?' he cried, as he disappeared from Wallace's sight.

'What is it?'

Douglas had his torch in his pocket and he reached for it. 'I slipped on something and I've hit something.' He flicked the torch on and gasped.

'Oh no!' exclaimed Wallace, as he climbed aboard to see by his brother's torchlight the sight of Ming lying on his back in a pool of his own blood. In one hand he was gripping a large knife and on each wrist was a horrific gash, the source of the blood.

Ming's staring eyes and the curious, fixed half-smile on his face suggested to them that he had found comfort in taking his own life.

'Bloody hell, Wallace, his blood is still pumping out! That means he still has a pulse. He's still alive.'

'Come on, you apply pressure and I'll phone Ralph McLelland. We'll save him yet.'

Torquil's phone vibrated in his jacket pocket and he immediately braked and cruised to a halt. He turned off the engine to answer the phone.

It was Wallace with the news of their discovery.

'Good grief!' he exclaimed. 'Well, that makes it all fit together, I suppose. No need for me to head for his house . . . Ralph has taken him to the cottage hospital and the psychiatrist has arrived from Lewis? . . . Good. I'll be back as soon as I can.'

Once he ended the call he tried to call Lorna, but she wasn't answering. So he tried Morag.

And she wasn't answering either.

Then he started to get worried.

He kicked the Bullet into action and wheeled round, then within moments he was hurtling along the road towards the manse.

VI

Cora and Calum had been taking it in turns to move the dummy every ten minutes.

Cora was starting to get quite worried. 'Do you think we ought to just lock the office door?' she whispered. 'I'm worried that we might both nod off.'

'It'll be fine, darling,' he said softly. 'Trust me, it will work like a charm. We just need to be patient.'

Cora yawned and grasped the golf club firmly. 'But I am not sure — '

There was the distinct rattle of the office doorhandle.

'Calum! Did you hear that?' she breathed.

Calm had already shot to his feet and grabbed his shinty stick. 'Aye, and I'm going to get him,' he whispered. 'Count to three, then hit the lights and then watch me do my stuff.'

Cora obeyed and hit the lights in time to see Calum hurtle down the stairs three at a time, howling like a banshee with his shinty stick whirling above his head.

She saw him vault the last few steps and land poised to strike.

But there was no one there.

VII

Crusoe's bark from downstairs had woken the Padre. He rose, switched on the light, threw on his dressing-gown and donned his slippers before heading for the stairs. He was halfway down when he heard an insistent banging on the front door.

Crusoe had gone running from his basket and was jumping up and down with his tail wagging back and forth.

'Are you all right, Lachlan?' Lorna's voice came through the letterbox.

'Of course I'm all right,' he returned, unlocking the door to reveal Lorna and Morag standing outside.

'I — er — I forgot my key,' Lorna said lamely.

'Why are there two of you? Not that I'm not delighted to see you too, Morag Discoll.'

He held the door open for them to come in, then ushered them through to the sitting room, where he switched on the light.

'Now, what is the problem?'

Morag's phone went off and she excused herself to go out into the hall to answer it while Lorna explained about Ming McDonald having absconded from the hospital and the call they received after he had gone to bed.

A few moments later Morag re-entered and told them about Ming having been found by the Drummonds.

'Wallace has let Torquil know and he's heading back to the station.'

Suddenly, Crusoe started to bark again. Almost immediately there was the sound of a

263

motorbike and then the scrunch of its wheels on the gravel outside.

'Thank goodness you are all OK!' Torquil said instants later as he came running in. 'I couldn't get you on either of your phones.'

'But at least we now know where Ming McDonald is,' said Morag. 'So there can't be a threat to Tam MacOnachie or anyone else. We can bring Ewan back in.'

The Padre nodded. 'Would anyone like a cocoa, or maybe something a wee bit stronger?'

VIII

Mellisa Mathieson woke with a thundering headache. She felt cold and frightened because she could not move a muscle or see. It seemed that something was covering her eyes and something was preventing her from opening her mouth. She quickly realized that she was bound hand and foot and was lying on a hard, cold floor with her head and neck propped up on some sort of pillow or cushion.

She struggled to move, sensing that she was naked.

And then she heard a throaty laugh that made her cringe and set her heart racing in terror.

14

I

It was quarter past midnight and Nettie Grant and the others were getting worried.

They had all agreed to meet again at her house for another séance at midnight to try and calm the spirits of Janet Horne and Henry Dodds, who, they were sure, were in turmoil. Both Agnes and Iona had felt them up by the Sentinel Stone, but the scepticism of Jerome Morton had acted as a barrier for them to come through properly, hence the reactions they had experienced.

Only, Melissa Mathieson had not shown up and she was not answering her phone. They had even gone to her shop, but it and the house behind were all in darkness and there was no answer to their knocking. Her car was still parked in the private space beside the shop.

Nettie had phoned the police station.

Ewan had gone back to the station from Tam MacOnachie's to await further instruction from Torquil and he answered her call.

'Something is wrong, Constable McPhee, I

know it,' Nettie said. 'We all know it and it is bad!'

Ewan promised to alert Inspector McKinnon and asked her and her friends in the meanwhile to stay together and go back to her house.

Torquil listened to Ewan as he relayed the message.

'They are convinced it has something to do with the killer, sir.'

'Frankly, Ewan, so am I. Ring the boys and tell them to come in and be on stand-by.'

'What are you going to do, Torquil?'

'I'm going to make an important phone call.'

II

Melissa had no idea how long she had been lying there since she heard the last peal of what seemed like insane laughter: she estimated about half an hour. For most of the time she was just aware of a humming and a bubbling, as if some sort of pump was in action somewhere nearby. She was also aware of the strong smell of brine.

Suddenly she heard footsteps and then sensed that someone was standing over her.

'Want to see the light, bitch?' a harsh voice snarled.

She felt a moment of pain as duct tape was ripped from across her eyes. She blinked repeatedly until gradually a blurred figure came into view. She recognized the man and then, worse, she realized that he was holding a speargun in his gloved hand. It was pointed at her chest.

'So sorry if you are feeling the cold,' Gavin McIntyre said, without a trace of genuine sorrow. 'It's just that I am going to need you to be naked later.'

Melissa Mathieson's heart was beating so fast she imagined that it could soon burst. But, at the realization that she was the prisoner of a madman who had stripped her clothing from her and tied her up, her eyes opened wide with alarm and fear as to what he meant. She shook her head vigorously.

Gavin McIntyre laughed. 'Oh don't worry, *Doctor* Mathieson. I'm not going to rape you. You are not my type. I am gay, you see.'

If Melissa was any less alarmed by that she didn't show it. Her eyes were fixed on the loaded speargun that he had trained on her heart.

'I'll make you a deal,' he went on. 'I'll take the duct tape off your mouth if you promise not to scream. I want to have a quiet chat with you. And anyway, there is no one within miles of us, so it wouldn't do any good. It would just make me angry, and you don't want to do that!'

She nodded and then braced herself as he yanked the tape from her mouth.

'That's better, *Doctor Mathieson*, isn't it?' he said, emphasizing the title again. 'You call yourself that, don't you, although you probably haven't even got a certificate in first aid.'

'I . . . I am a doctor in radionics and angel therapy.'

'Bullshit! You are a quack. A dangerous quack who kills people, like my partner Fernando Rodriquez. He believed all your garbage remedies would cure his cancer. But it didn't! It spread to his bones and still he took your useless medicines and told me about those invisible angels that he said brought healing energy.'

Melissa fought to bring the patient notes to mind. She had a vague recollection, but fear of the speargun made thinking difficult.

'I . . . I don't remember clearly,' she said hesitantly.

'Wrong answer!' he thundered, his hand visibly shaking on the speargun that he held in his right hand.

'I'm sorry. So sorry,' she sobbed. Please . . . please don't kill me.'

He looked at the speargun and laughed. 'Yeah, you ought to be scared of this thing. I used it to kill that stupid Henry Dodds character.'

Melissa gasped. 'You k-killed him? Why?'

'Because the stupid fool was up on the moor when you lot were holding that vigil you kindly told the world about on the news. I had burgled the chandlery and knocked it about to make it look as if a nutter was loose, and I took this baby. I had seen it in there earlier when Murdoch and I were interviewing MacOnachie. Anyway, I was making my way up the Sentinel Stone and he came across me. He was pissed and told me that he was going up to see you. He was babbling about love at first sight. Then he saw the speargun that I was going to shoot you with and his sozzled mind managed to put two and two together. He realized there was something odd about a bloke wandering about on a moor with a speargun in the middle of the night.'

He sighed. 'So he just had to go. He looked really surprised when I shot him through the heart. Then I dragged him into the bushes and left the sign of Sagittarius, the archer, on a stone.' He laughed, 'That was a neat little touch, don't you think?'

'Are . . . are you the one who has been sending me those emails?' she asked, tremulously.

'Of course that was me! I hated you after Fernando died and I had tried to get my anger at you out of my system by writing a cookery book. A book on sushi, as it happens.' He looked around him and laughed. 'How ironic that is, when we have ended up here.'

Then he noticed that she did not understand. 'Oh, don't worry, love. You'll understand only too well in a few minutes.'

He waved the speargun at her. 'Oh yes, about the emails, when I decided that I needed to teach you a lesson, a very final lesson, I started sending them through a dark hole in the Internet. It was a way of softening you up, or tenderizing you before the kill, so to speak.'

His eyes hardened. 'But then when I saw you after that lecture, down by the harbour, I kind of flipped and I just wanted to kill you. To smash the life out of you. I grabbed a bottle that some drunk had conveniently left on the harbour wall and smashed your head.'

Suddenly he looked wistful, almost apologetic.

'Only it wasn't you, was it? It was that equally loopy Dr Horne. She looked just like you in the moonlight. When I realized my mistake I dropped her into the water and scrawled that Aquarius sign on the wall.'

He laughed. 'And then those imbeciles at

the *Chronicle* started the story about the zodiac killer. And I guess that Calum Steele's little podcast scared you as much as it prompted me to take action tonight.'

'I was petrified that you were going to come for me,' Melissa volunteered. 'And I thought that if they knew who you were I ought to go and talk to them. I thought that I might be safer with them than on my own, and that I could persuade them to get the police to arrest you straight away, rather than in the morning.'

'You really believe that they know anything?' He tossed his head back and laughed. 'They know nothing. It was a stupid bluff, don't you see?'

He frowned. 'But why didn't you just go to the police and ask them for protection in the first place?'

Melissa bent her head. 'I . . . I didn't dare. I have a record.'

'A record! For what, killing another patient?'

She shook her head. 'Nothing like that. I was young and stupid. I embezzled a charity I worked for. I couldn't risk exposing myself. It would have ruined everything.'

He laid the speargun aside with a sigh. 'No matter. But now it's your turn, *Doctor* Mathieson. We've had Aquarius and Sagittarius so now I think it will be Scorpio. I'm

271

afraid that we haven't got any scorpions, but the sting of jellyfish should do rather nicely.'

He stopped and hefted her roughly onto his shoulder and walked towards one of the large tanks. He held her over it and let her see the masses of huge jellyfish of many different colours.

'This is all thanks to that lunatic fisherman and his crank theory. I have mixed them all together so that they should make a nice cold collation of poisonous venom. There should be enough poison in there to stop your heart and freeze your brain — after an age of agonizing pain. I believe that their stings are extremely painful.'

He laughed as she started screaming and struggled for all she was worth.

'Now you can see why I had to take the liberty of undressing you, don't you? Every inch of your body is going to experience pain, so that you get an inkling of what it is like to feel the pain that you made Fernando suffer.'

He hefted her further up on his shoulder and was about to launch her when a strong hand yanked him backwards and then pulled Melissa off his shoulder.

Gavin McIntyre spun round just in time to have the vague impression of Inspector Torquil McKinnon's fist hurtling towards him. It connected with his jaw and lifted him

272

bodily off his feet to go crashing in a heap against the side of the tank.

'You're not killing anybody today,' Torquil said, as he handcuffed the unconscious man before covering Melissa Mathieson's naked body with his leather jacket.

'You should have come to us, Dr Mathieson,' he said. 'But you are safe now. I'll see if I can find your clothes.'

Melissa could barely speak, she was trembling so much. 'He . . . he was going to throw me in there. Inspector McKinnon, I don't know how to thank you.'

'No thanks are necessary. I'll need you to make a full statement, of course. And I mean about everything, including your own record that you mentioned.'

'You heard me tell him?'

Torquil patted his pocket. 'I have it all recorded on my phone.'

Gavin McIntyre groaned and then opened his eyes. When he saw Melissa and Torquil he tried to sit up, only then realizing that he was handcuffed. He slumped back against the tank.

'Gavin McIntyre,' Torquil said, 'I am arresting you on suspicion of having committed the murder of two people. You do not have to say anything, but it may harm your defence if you do not mention when questioned something which you later rely on in court. Anything you do say may be used in evidence.'

McIntyre said nothing.

III

Two days later the whole island was still in a state of shock, but gradually life was getting back to normal.

Superintendent Lumsden allowed Lorna to stay on to help clear up all the reports and loose ends that resulted from the arrest and the preparation for the court case.

The Padre cooked one of his special seafood paellas for Torquil's team. They sat round the large dining-room table and relaxed in the ambience of the manse, enjoying Lachlan's cooking accompanied by some very good Portuguese vinho verde.

'Tell me, Torquil,' Lachlan asked, 'how did you know that McIntyre was the killer?'

Torquil dabbed his mouth with his napkin. 'I didn't until it occurred to me that he hadn't mentioned anything about Ming's jellyfish collection. It had been bothering me for a while, I think. Then when we got the news that Melissa Mathieson had gone missing it made me suspicious that the killer was still on the loose and that she was going to be his next victim. I phoned the hotel and asked to be put through to Gavin McIntyre. Then, when there was no answer, I got them to check if he was actually in his room and, of course, it was empty. Then it all made sense. He hadn't mentioned anything because he had probably planned to use not only the jellyfish, but Ming's place to take her to as well. I guess he would have had an idea of dealing with Ming and putting the blame on him anyway, but when Ming had his breakdown it must have seemed like a blessing to him. The use of jellyfish stings would have given him a reason to leave a Scorpio symbol and keep the zodiac killer idea going.'

'I am guessing that he will go away for a very long time,' Morag said. She shook her head. 'I feel sorry for Melissa Mathieson. She must have been utterly terrified.'

Torquil nodded. 'She was also terrified about her friends discovering that she had a criminal conviction. I wonder how they will take that?'

'If they are real friends they will accept her for who she is now, not for what she did when she was young,' said Lorna.

'And she did pay for the crime with a prison sentence, didn't she?' Lachlan pointed out.

'That's right,' Torquil replied. She served

six months in prison for embezzlement from a charity she worked for ten years ago. She had thought that by coming to West Uist she could build a totally new identity. She had thought that was the crime he had referred to in one of his emails.'

'Poor Ming McDonald,' said Ewan. 'I hope he'll be all right. And to think that everyone thought he was the killer.'

'Ralph McLelland was going to come tonight, but he's got a confinement to attend to,' Torquil said. 'But he says that Ming is doing well over in the psychiatric unit on Lewis. Apparently he had built up a whole delusional system around Tam MacOnachie. It seems that in a lucid moment he felt incredibly guilty about cutting the buoys out at the Cruadalach Isles and that had flipped him and made him feel suicidal.'

Morag squeezed Douglas's arm. 'I'm sorry that it didn't work out with Rosie Barton.'

Douglas grinned sheepishly. 'Och, that is just one of those things. She and Jerome had unfinished business. I'll be fine in a few days.'

'Besides, we have a fishing business that has been neglected lately,' quipped Wallace. 'All those fish in the sea are waiting for us.'

'Did you all read Calum Steele's latest issue of the *Chronicle?*' Morag asked. 'The chap is unbelievable. He was not at all fazed by the trouble he stirred up and he still claimed that he had been on the verge of revealing who the murderer was. More than that, he claimed that the *Chronicle* had been instrumental in bringing the zodiac killer to justice.'

'That's my old friend Calum, for you,' said Torquil. 'He had the hide of a rhinoceros when he was at school and, if anything, it has just grown thicker over the years.'

'That's not the case with Murdoch Jamieson,' the Padre said. 'He was distraught to think that his business partner was a cold-blooded murderer. He retired forthwith and says that there will be no more *Heavens Above* ever filmed again.'

'I must say, I think that I for one have had enough of these celestial events,' said Lorna.

The Padre held up his hand. 'I agree, but it is time for one last celestial event. I've made a special star-fruit sundae for you all.'

He laughed and raised his glass. 'And here's to all of you. You are all superstars in my eyes.'

We do hope that you have enjoyed reading this large print book.

Did you know that all of our titles are available for purchase?

We publish a wide range of high quality large print books including:
Romances, Mysteries, Classics
General Fiction
Non Fiction and Westerns

Special interest titles available in large print are:
The Little Oxford Dictionary
Music Book
Song Book
Hymn Book
Service Book

Also available from us courtesy of Oxford University Press:
Young Readers' Dictionary
(large print edition)
Young Readers' Thesaurus
(large print edition)

For further information or a free brochure, please contact us at:
Ulverscroft Large Print Books Ltd.,
The Green, Bradgate Road, Anstey,
Leicester, LE7 7FU, England.
Tel: (00 44) 0116 236 4325
Fax: (00 44) 0116 234 0205

FLOTSAM & JETSAM

Keith Moray

The Flotsam & Jetsam TV show gained a cult following throughout Scotland by highlighting that money could be made from the debris that washed up onto remote beaches. When it came to West Uist, it brought the exciting prospect of celebrity status for the locals. Then, one fateful night, everything changed . . . The death of a noted scientist, the discovery of a half-drowned puppy and the suggestion of police negligence now lead Inspector Torquil McKinnon to investigate sinister events on the seemingly idyllic island. Who knows what other secrets will be washed ashore?

MURDER SOLSTICE

Keith Moray

Museum curator Finlay MacNeil had spent years trying to decipher the markings on the Hoolish Stones, the stone circle which for millennia had stood on the West Uist. He was suspicious of the cult-like group at Dunshiffin Castle, which was preparing to celebrate the summer solstice. It seemed that his fatal mistake was to challenge their beliefs on Scottish TV. Yet Inspector Torquil McKinnon had many other things on his mind. So when attractive Sergeant Lorna Golspie arrived on the island to investigate the way he ran his station, was it enough to distract him from the forthcoming Murder Solstice?